TIMELESS TALES TOLD

DAMSELS OVERCOME

Feminist Empowerment

Bobbie Kinkead

As Is Production for BobbieTales
San Francisco, Bay Area, California

ISBNs:
Paperback: 987-1-942070-05-4
Hardcover: 978-1-942070-08-5
ePub: 987-1-942070-06-1
Kindle: 978-1-942070-07-8
Audio: 987-1-942070-09-2

Library of Congress Control Number: 2021901204

Pick any folktale…enhance, elaborate, reimage, fabricate, embroidery, and adapt. Write with a different setting: today, ancient time, in space, another country. Add characters or change their names, or modify, reimage, adapt, embroidery, embellish, fabricate, or elaborate the ones in the story. Remember, traditional folktales have no copyright and create a significant jump for a story plot. Look at the different versions on the websites, movies, videos, or books. The stories change through the years and places; Cinderella is an excellent example of having many variations and interpretations.

Give credit to your sources. Please, all storytellers, picture book authors, middle-grade authors, YA authors, and adult novelists, list at least three sources used to write, or tell, or film a story. We want and need respect for our translations, creativity adaptations, and structure of characters, place, time, and plots in our stories, even from the oldest traditional, classic folktales, legends, myths, fables, and fairytales.

Publisher's Note: although many edits made on the context, mistakes might be found.

Dedication

For all females and males today and tomorrow:

My realization: all traditional tales between the twelfth to eighteenth centuries written by male voices dominated classic literature, even today, to keep the male norms. Selected are folktales from my child reading and adult storytelling, which influence my thinking that "wo<u>men</u> are the servers, helpless, evil, hysterical, not worthy, the weaker sex" as truth and influenced my reality. This collection of folktales is about wo<u>men</u> who inspire. The powers of the females in *Damsels Overcome* reveal their skills used to survive as dames, dolls, heroines, females, ladies, lassies, matrons, maids, maidens, women, or crones. Included are bits of my opinions about the traditional male norms. These folktales and legends I have enhanced, adapted, and re-imaged into female narratives where possible.

As I discovered, males are also victims of these norms.

Especially, gigantic thanks to my husband, Don, whose grandmother was a suffragette, and who understands the equality of men and women. I am blessed to have him.

Table of Contents

BEING

Let go of the "he" in she also her, the "male" in female and woman, and say and write, BEING who has a SELF called I, my, mine, and me. The male is only half of any being and not to dominate over the other half, the human.

Let us restructure our thinking.

Self as being
who trusts and respects.

Self as being
who heals the past.

Self as being
who heals the present.

Self a being
who uses given talents.

Self as being
who is the accumulation of wisdom.

Self as being
who values other beings, and
maintains the truths about others.

This being is you and me.
We accept our abundance.
We own our skills.
We trust our powers.
We love others as equals.

BEING affirms life.

1

Oak and the Reeds an Aesop's fable

Hear a story!
Read a story!
Write a story!
Understand the story!
Male narratives promote their norms!

Oak and the Reeds

A magnificent Oak stood proudly by a quiet pool, and at its feet grew a cluster of modest and slender reeds. Whenever a high wind blew, the tree stood firm as a mountain, reaching its limbs high into the sky. The reeds could only bend and bow.

"No wind can ever make me bow my head," said the proud Oak.

"Wait and see," whispered the reeds as they swayed with the wind, "wait and see."

Soon came a furious storm. The reeds were shaken and tossed in the gust this way and that way. The mighty Oak stood tall and straight defying the storm. The wind came faster and more ferocious. At last, the Oak's roots tore from the ground; the tree fell with a crash.

After the storm passed in the morning light, the reeds stood tall. "You see!" They said softly to the falling Oak. "We bowed to the wind, and we survived. You resisted and perished."

Why power in flexibility?

The folktales included in this book reveal positions used by women as damsels to survive the male norms, who had the POWER. Maidens, matrons, and crones — are mere females, who solved the problems and dilemmas in their time. For eons, social norms were taught through folktales and legends written by males with their views of dominance. I once believed this authority the truth, valid, dictating my attitude that only males were authors or artists.

As a child, the only stories I heard were fishing and hunting stories told by my dad or what my mom told about her relations. So, I made up my stories. As a teenager, I travelled with my friend, Marion, to the West Side Library in Colorado City to check out every fairytale, folktale, myth, and legend I could. Later in my life, I told Asian stories at the Asian Art Museum in San Francisco, learning the history of oral cultures. Most, maybe all the stories recorded were written by males. When I realized this, I was appalled.

Clever, wise, powerful females need roles in stories as leading positive characters that overcome tyranny and suppression, not to submit helplessly. Survival is essential and so are worth and value.

Yesterday, as today, I am still treated as second-class as included in these words: fe<u>male</u>, <u>lady</u>, wo<u>man</u>, <u>she</u> or <u>her</u>, and <u>her</u>oine. Dictionaries are male-dominated; check out the words. Males are also damsels caught in the norms they protect.

In this collection of folktales and legends, I rewrote the stories into female narratives to understand what females felt as they bowed to the social winds. The reeds were flexible and bent under the power of the wind and cast their seeds. And so, the damsels show how they survived male norms and the skills I learned from them to bend and succeed. Only, I am tired of bending.

2

Naga Princess enhanced

The boys pounded sticks on the ground to scare a naga as she slid away. She raised her head this way and that way, hissing. Then the sticks hit her head and pounded against her body.

The naga saw BoSinh walking by the field. He watched the boys.

Raising her head in his direction, she hissed. *"Help me. HELP ME!* The boys want to kill me; I have children within."

BoSinh walked to the boys. "I will pay coins for the snake." The boys still beat the snake as she slid to the bushes. BoSinh reached into his pocket and showed his coins. The boys dropped their sticks, took the coins, and raced to the market.

The naga slid from the bushes to bow to BoSinh, hissing, "I am a Princess Naga, daughter of the Naga King. You saved my life and my children; I will be forever grateful." She slid into the bushes.

A few moons later, BoSinh went to the funeral of a friend bitten by a naga and died. BoSinh grieved his best friend. He forgot he saved the Princess Naga; he hated snakes.

One day on the entrance step into his hut, two nagas were coiled sleeping in the warmth of the sun. BoSinh picked up a stick and beat on the steps scaring the snakes from their sleep. In hatred, he yelled, "You're worthless, off my step. You bit my friend. He died because of your poison. Killers!" He threw the stick at the nagas to hurt them.

As the two nagas slipped from the step into the bushes, one hissed, "We won't forget this. We revenge you, who throws hatred." They slithered into the bushes.

The next day, while BoSinh worked in the rice field, the two nagas slipped into his hut and hid in the wooded rafters waiting for his return.

The Naga Princess heard from relatives about the revenge of the two nagas on BoSinh, who saved her. She went to the hut appearing as a young maiden.

"*Knock, Knock.*" The maiden waited.

BoSinh opened the door, surprised to see a young maiden standing on his step.

"I'm the Naga Princess," she bowed. "BoSinh, you saved my life many months ago from the boys in the rice field."

"You are a young maiden?"

"BoSinh, all animals may appear as humans to talk to humans; you are the highest being. I come to repay your kindness, to save your life."

The maiden looked into the rafters and called, "Cousins, come down."

Two nagas looked down. "Princess Naga, the day before, BoSinh tried to kill us with a stick, yelling *poisonous*! We revenge him."

The maiden pointed to the floor. The two nagas slid down a beam hissing at BoSinh and bowed to the Naga Princess. She motioned them to bow to BoSinh. They did not.

The maiden asked BoSinh, "Why do you hate nagas; you saved my life and my children within me?"

"A snake's venom killed my best friend."

"Snakes are poisonous to those who have a reason. We are not to know why."

BoSinh listened and looked at the nagas.

The maiden continued, "Human's mouths are poisonous. They cause pain, hatred, and death to others by the words they speak. Not only snakes have venom."

"I never thought of words as poison."

The Naga Princess motioned the nagas to bow to BoSinh. They nodded to the maiden, not to BoSinh.

The maiden asked, "BoSinh, forgive my cousins?"

BoSinh would not bow to the snakes.

"Forget your hatred for each other. Tell the other snakes not to threaten BoSinh."

BoSinh bowed to the two nagas.

The two bowed to BoSinh and slid out the door into the bushes.

The maiden asked, "May I come back? We must talk more to answer questions about nagas."

"I will wait for your visit."

Days later, the Naga Princess brought her youngest sister to visit BoSinh. Day after day, the three talked about why animals took human form.

"We learn from the highest of creation, the humans, who cannot be animals."

BoSinh said, "I never desire to be an animal."

From that time on, the naga sisters appeared as humans, and BoSinh forgot they were nagas.

Many moons later, the King of Nagas sent a note to BoSinh asking him to take his younger daughter as his wife. BoSinh, although honored, answered, "I no longer hate nagas and have a better understanding of all creatures. I am a human and cannot live with a naga as a wife."

The Naga Princesses visited BoSinh.

"My sister and I became humans when we spoke to you as now. My sister can live with you as a human. As you know, nagas may improve themselves."

BoSinh said, "I agree to marry your sister if she remains human." The young maiden agreed. They lived happily in the mountains and raised a beautiful family.

After BoSinh and his wife died, their children built an altar for them. For many years, their children noticed a long naga curled around the incense burner at the anniversary for their parents.

◆◆◆◆◆◆

Why power in education?

As I told the naga's sister in the Asia Art Museum I understood why education is insightful, informative, and awareness. As a young female youth, I attended the University of Colorado and learned the male social structure as a mere female. Feminists were not outspoken in Colorado, even though one of the first states to allow women settlers to vote, enticing them to live in Colorado as wives, servants, or "ladies of the night."

♦♦♦♦♦♦♦

In the Eastern half of our globe, the snake, naga, symbolizes emotions to be honored, although controlled. A snake did tempt Eve, the emotional side of humans. Today, many women are afraid of snakes and must maintain that attitude at costs their inequality. Males are in control; the farmer in the story teaches and educates his wife; he is supreme and honored being above all animals. Notice the male has a name, BoSinh. Men receive adoration from the women in these ancient traditional tales. Although the young naga has hopes in human education, I think being a naga would be more fun.

Rabbit in the Moon
re-imaged

Tonight, heavy rains fell on the trees. A cold storm hid the moon behind the clouds while lightning and thunder boomed through the valley. A pretty brown Rabbit cooked in a hut against the mountain. She was alert for *DANGER*. Long ears observed sounds and a twitching nose tested the smells.

She wore an apron; a cooking spoon in hand stirred soup in a pot hung from the stones in the fireplace. The flames crackled and spit sparks into the room as the rain dropped down the chimney. Fruits readied for her friend Monkey and roasted mouse for her friend Fox. Rabbit loved to care for her friends.

Sitting at a wooden table was Monkey, a jittery fellow with a worried face and brown eyes, which were wide, open. The storm was too windy for him. He walked over to Rabbit, looked into the pot, then walked back to the table and sat, only to repeat walking to Rabbit, who gently smiled at him.

On the other side of the table stood Fox. He was older and wise, gaining knowledge from his hunts. He liked the night; only this night came with a storm. Fox, irritated by the blowing wind and pounding rain, pranced around the small room, and sat, only to prance around the room again. Rabbit patted Fox as he passed by.

Both waited for their supper. The smells were so delicious; one could taste the fragrance. Rabbit cooked the best foods that were seasoned just right. Both liked living with Rabbit, who also served them by washing and folding their clothes. She loved to clean, she made their beds and swept, she tended the garden. She brought in the vegetables and chopped them for her tasty soups. Both ate well. Monkey did help with the fruit trees and did a bit of gardening. Fox did bring in bugs, fish, and a mouse now and then for Rabbit to cook.

Tonight, the Sky God looked down on Mother Earth. "I wonder if there is a creature that would serve me beyond what anyone could imagine?" Having said this, the Sky God transformed as a beggar. His hair messed and greasy; a long rugged beard dirtied with rotten foods. His feet wrapped with rags. Worse, he smelled of old sweat and rotten meat, and his eyes red and face wrinkled.

He climbed down an enormous Pine tree in a beautiful forest on a mountain in Japan. He looked through the tall, thick trees and noticed a wooden hut built against the mountain stone. The rains poured, and the wind pushed the trees as the old beggar approached the hut. The enticing flavors filled the air and convinced the Sky God that he must visit the shabby, although attended, clean, and nice hut. He liked the garden.

Bang! Bang! Bang! The beggar almost broke the door.

The harsh noise scared Fox and Monkey; they ran around the table, clutching each other. Rabbit looked up from stirring the pot of soup. She looked over at Fox, being the bravest. Rabbit ordered, "Fox, go open the door."

"*No!*" said Fox, "I'm not going to open the door, *No*! Who knows what beast lurks, ready to eat us. I've seen such things in the dark shadow waiting, creeping."

Rabbit chucked, "Oh, go, Fox, we will never know. Open the door. Whoever is outside is cold and needs help."

Fox slowly crept to the door while Monkey climbed to the top of the rafters into his special place where he peeked down, silent.

When the door opened, a gushing wind pushed Fox to the floor, followed by splashing rain. Into the hut stumbled a decrepit, dirty, unkempt human, wet, and smelling of rot.

The three animals watched, petrified.

Finally, Rabbit offered, "What may we do for you?"

"I need warmth and food."

The beggar entered the room and sat at the table. Monkey's eyes, large and scared, said, "I will get fruits."

Coming back inside, the wind and rain following, Monkey said, "Too cold, too wild, I brought a few green soybeans."

The beggar looked at Fox, "I need more than these to eat."

Fox offered, "Here is my roasted mouse. Or, I will catch fish."

Rushing back inside, Fox said, "Too windy and cold for fishing. Here are some bugs."

"Mice and bugs will make me sick."

Rabbit offered, "Cooked on this stick, they will be tasty."

The old beggar moved closer to the fire and roasted the bugs. He ate the mouse.

"I need more!"

Rabbit looked at her friends, who cowered; the smells of fright overwhelmed the scent of the fire and soup.

Fox whispered to Rabbit, "He wants to eat us."

"He will not. Get my biggest pot that hangs outside."

"Monkey! Climb down and go outside and pick a head of cabbage, a daikon, eggplant, more soybeans, and ginger root and bring herbs hanging on the hut."

Both left the door open; wind and rain pounded inside. The old beggar cringed with cold. Rabbit saw Fox and Monkey talking outside. She feared they would run away.

She called, "Monkey, put the vegetables in the pot. Then gather firewood."

"Fox, bring the pot with the vegetables inside."

Both came inside, carrying their loads. Fox dumped the pot with vegetables on the table; Monkey dropped the wood by the fire. Both glared at Rabbit.

Rabbit scorned, "Fox, you fill the pot with our soup and add more water." He sat in a corner, refusing to move.

"Monkey, put wood on the fire." He climbed up the wall into his hiding place and stared down.

Rabbit built a hotter fire for the beggar.

"The warmth is good; I'm getting dry, only starving."

In a bucket of water, she washed the carrots and daikon, then sliced them. She chopped the cabbage and eggplant and grated the ginger into the pot. Rabbit cut and chopped, saying nothing.

The soybeans she put on a plate by the beggar.

Then, taking the dirty water out, she watered the vegetables and added their skins to the mulch. Rabbit noticed a light rain fell, and a quiet wind blew.

She poured the soup from the small pot into the large pot, added water, and then added each cut vegetable. Rabbit watched the beggar and her friends.

Monkey hid; Rabbit could hear his fearful sniffing. Fox walked around in an angrily, frightening matter.

Appetizing smells swelled inside the hut; the soup ready to eat.

Fox approached and whispered. "Rabbit, he wants to eat us."

Rabbit placed three bowls on the table with rice cakes, then directed. "Fox and Monkey sit on this side of the table. The beggar will have his soup."

She bowed to the beggar and slowly to her friends.

With a quick jump, Rabbit splashed into the hot pot of soup.

Fox and Monkey gasped, then screamed, holding each other. The beggar became the Sky God, rushed to the pot, pulled Rabbit out, opened the hut door, and hurled Rabbit up onto the moon with a powerful thrust.

Turning to Rabbit's friends, the Sky God said, "Rabbit is the most generous and powerful spirit I know. She gave her life, saving you from your fears. Rabbit will always remain on the moon to remind us how much she deserves praise."

Why serving is strength?

I assumed, because the Moon is associated with female power, every woman knew Rabbit is our symbol for a healer, server; she is our power symbol. I was horrified to find this tale narrated in a male voice, and the rabbit was a male.

Women worshipped both Rabbit and the Moon as symbols of fertility, fruitfulness, abundance, sexuality, procreation, renewal, spring, growth, and love. Rabbit symbolizes the receptacle of souls between life and death associated with the Moon. Both women and rabbit participate in the time cycles: growth, decline, destruction, and the menstrual cycles (the Moon cycles).

When I told my version in the Japanese Gallery at Asia Art Museum in San Francisco, I changed the gender to a female and her narrative. I put the god in the middle of the story, not the beginning, as usual in folktales—this is a female tale.

+ + ◆ + + +

One never knows by looking at a rabbit—the gender could be male or female. In today's world, both help and serve others, one of the greatest gifts. Something happens, a tragedy, DOOM. Spontaneously, *BAM*, someone appears to support life. Besides, we feel good when giving and serving. We share!

+ + ◆ + + +

When I was a child in Colorado, rabbits jumped in the prairies as we drove across. Rabbits hunted by the early settlers provided food and skins for warmth. I loved watching the rabbits munch on leaves of the wild plants while I fished with my brother and dad.

Rabbit was my symbol while painting at an easel or sitting while writing my picture story; she is my month in the Chinese Zodiac, the server. I did create and illustrate a story about a rabbit in *Vannita and the Basket of Eggs*. The young female New York editors had no understanding or appreciation of Rabbit as the honored and respected Goddess; they only saw the painted fertile eggs offered to children as a horror. Farmers do offer brooding hens fertile eggs to hatch. Young editors schooled in the male-dominated social norms accept his narrative. I did not realize this lost connection when I submitted Vannita.

Notes about Rabbit

Rabbit and the Moon exists in folklore from Anglo-Saxon, Greek, United Kingdom, Chinese, the *Buddhist Jataka Tales*, the Japanese anthology *Konjaku Monogatarishū*, and Aztec mythology.

In ancient Anglo-Saxon mythology Ostara is the rising sun, depicted with a Hare's head or ears that are associated with the spring and fertility and resurrection. She is the friend of all children, and she changes her pet bird into a rabbit to amuse them. This rabbit brought forth brightly colored eggs, which the Goddess gave to the children as gifts. The day of Easter emerges from the German Eostre, pagan tradition, the Goddess of the dawn, bringer of light, Goddess of fertility whose animal symbol was a bunny, known for energetic breeding—thus has traditionally symbolized fertility. Since that time, Rabbit appeared on the Moon because of feminine, strong lunar associations.

Ostara is identical to the Greek Eos and the Roman Aurora and her name is related to "estrus," a woman's sexual organ for birthing. Ostara is often a companion to Cupid and an attribute of Aphrodite/Venus.

In the United Kingdom, the Hare was sacred to the moon goddess Andraste, and hare hunting was a common Easter activity in England.

Hittavainen (or Hittauanin) is the Karelian god of Hares and hare hunting.

The Norse goddess Freyja had Hare attendants.

Hare is associated with the Celtic goddess Cerridwen.

Kaltes is the moon goddess of the Ugric people in western Siberia across Asia cultures and appears as a shape-shifter; she manifested as a Hare, sacred to her.

Pn'gau, the first Dragon, died and his body created China. His left eye floated into the sky as the Moon, giving herbs to the people. While in the Moon, Rabbit ground the spices and herbs for the early medicines. Later, the Chinese God of Farming changed Rabbit into a Goddess who gave medicines to the people of China.

In the Buddhist Jataka teaching tale (Tale 316), [3], about 3000 years ago, Rabbit was the first of five hundred reincarnations before finally born as Buddha. After the full Moon, there is a holy day when one gives to those less fortunate.

In Mexican folklore, an Aztec legend, God Quetzalcoatl, living on earth as a man after walking a long time, became hungry. With no food or water around, he would die. A nearby rabbit offered herself as food to save his life. Quetzalcoatl, moved by the rabbit's offering, said, "You may be just a rabbit, but everyone will remember you; your image in light (on the Moon) for people for all time."

Many male gods—Buddha, the Japanese Sun God, God Quetzalcoatl, and others—placed Rabbit in the Moon, their propagation for their male religious dominance to gain power over the Goddess in the Moon and the female server.

4

Spider Weaver exaggerated

A spider enjoyed the sunshine and played with a light ray on her web. A Japanese rice farmer named Yosaku rested on the rock, eating his lunch. She watched him eat and marveled that the man ate whitefly larvae smaller than the flies she ate.

All this time, a snake watched the spider watching Yosaku. The snake's tongue reached into the air, tasting the spider, his meal. Yosaku happened to see the snake ready to eat the spider as she jumped up and down on her web. The snake readied to pounce. Yosaku kicked his lunch containers, then flung his hoe at the snake, who hissed at Yosaku before slithering into the brush.

The spider hid in a crevice of a rock, watching while Yosaku put his containers back together. He did look for her. She stayed hidden, even though she was grateful that he saved her. She watched Yosaku walk to the rice field to work.

The spider waited for Yosaku to return. Later that night, he rested on the same rock by the stream. He noticed the web still hung there. From the rock, the spider crawled onto the hoe that leaned there. Yosaku picked up the hoe, not detecting the spider. His walk was long; he lived in the village. At the door, the spider jumped from the hoe onto the hut. Then she slid through a crack, climbing onto a rafter in the ceiling. She spun a web and sat comfortably. Yosaku did not notice her. Tomorrow, she would repay his kindness and protection of her.

Early the next morning, on the step into Yosaku's home, the spider turned herself into a human maiden. She was young, thin, energetic, beautiful, and dressed in farmer's clothing. Most uncomfortable having two arms and walking on two long legs, she tapped on the door.

Yosaku answered, surprised. He bowed, "Young maiden, what can I do for you?"

She bowed. From her throat, a voice came, "Not what you can, what I may do for you. Do you need a weaver?"

"Yes, I do. I have hemp to weave. I work all day."

"Show me to the weaving room, and I will work there. Only please don't watch me. I work better alone."

Yosaku walked the maiden to the weaving area stacked with hemp, ready to weave into floor mats. He hung baling that covered the hemp around the weaving area so the spider maiden could work in privacy. "I will return home later in the evening. Just leave the hemp mats where the bales are."

When Yosaku ate lunch that day in the same place, the spider was not there. Her web ripped apart. He feared the snake ate her. Yosaku saddened; he enjoyed watching the spider playing with the sunray on her web.

The spider maiden wove the hemp into six mats for floor coverings. She then crawled to her web and waited. Later that evening, when Yosaku entered the hut, the spider once again became a maiden and greeted him.

"I have finished the weaving; here are six mats for you."

Yosaku looked at the mats. "These are too fine for my use. I will sell them in the market."

The spider maiden humbly bowed. "If you buy cotton, I will weave for you."

"You need not."

"I must weave for gratitude to you."

The spider maiden left. From the porch, she became a spider crawling to the rafter to her web and watched. Yosaku happily inspected the mats he was to sell.

The next day, the spider watched Yosaku roll the mats, put them on his back, and disappear down the path. She played with the Sun and danced on a ray. She had a full lunch of flies and waited for Yosaku to return.

At the market, the traders were impressed with the hemp mats. Yosaku earned six gold coins. He watched the fun, ate delightful sushi, and had his share of Saki. He bought two large bales of cotton. He managed to get them on his back and walked carefully home. Needing a rest, he sat by the stream where the spider played with the sunray…her web empty and tattered.

In the bushes observing Yosaku crept the snake. Out of curiosity, the snake crawled into a bale of cotton. He wanted to see if the spider was with the farmer.

When Yosaku arrived home, he managed to get the two large bales into his hut and then into the small weaving area. While Yosaku rested, the spider waited, pleased with her secret. The snake patiently waited in the cotton.

The next morning, Yosaku woke up early, ready to work his rice field. The spider crept along the rafters to the wall onto the step of the hut. She changed into a young maiden again. She tapped on the door. "I'm here to weave the cotton for you."

Yosaku showed her the two bales and unwrapped the cotton.

The snake hid deep inside the bales; Yosaku was not aware.

"When you weave this cotton, I will have money for a long time." He bowed, "I am honored and pleased you want to help. May I repay you?"

The spider maiden bowed, "Wait to see the cloth tonight. Please do not watch me weaving." She slipped into the weaving area.

Yosaku was curious, so he crept to the hanging clothes to peek at the secret weaver. He gasped and held his mouth. Never did he imagine—the maiden was a spider. He watched as she ate the cotton; a string came from her orb. Yosaku watched, sick while curious. He said not a word as his eyes observed a small spider spin the yarn while her legs wove into wefts on the loom.

Astonished, Yosaku slowly backed away. He held great respect and was humbled. The spider honored him—the spider he saved from the snake. Weaving was her appreciation, her thanks for what he did. Such a fearless offer and such a powerful thank you. He quietly walked to his rice field.

The snake crawled from the cotton and watched the spider weave. She ate the last of the cotton; she was full and heavy.

The snake struck!

Spider Weaver jumped, slowly and awkwardly landing on the edge of the window. The snake flung himself upward and slid beside her. She jumped into the air.

He jumped!

A ray of light the spider caught climbing as fast as she could.

The snake fell into the dried leaves outside the hut.

Full of cotton, the spider slowly crawled up the ray. When reaching the sun, the spider, happy and grateful, wove what we know as clouds. The sun, overjoyed, called the clouds and the spider, Kumo.

As for Yosaku, when he came home, he found the cotton cloth woven as fine as silk and enough for eight kimonos. He assumed the spider returned to her web. At the market, the fabric sold for many, many gold coins. Yosaku lived well for the rest of his life and never forgot about the spider and her weaving for him.

Why giving gift has potential?

Flash! Spider Maiden does not have a name; she is only called "maiden." The male farmer has a reputation in classic traditional folktale from Japan's male-dominated society. During this time, women walked behind the male. At least the Sun, a female god, honored the Spider Maiden with a name, Kumo.

Gift giving for protection "for being taken care of" is what women do and did, yesterday and today in most cultures.

My mother wanted an education. Instead, her stepfather stopped her, claiming "Women only get married; their duties are to the family." At age fourteen, she worked in the home of another family, learning woman's skills. In older times, girls married off at age twelve "to be taken care of," an owned piece of property. She expected to give her gifts of children and service for male prosperity.

After many protests, thank goodness today, the anguished cries of women finally heard and laws passed, so the damsels are almost treated equally. Today's males, as partners, help with family tasks, providing women time to achieve as doctors, nurses, news forecasters, scientists, professors, politicians, lawyers, judges, or CEOs, or to run their own companies.

The protests and laws fought for by grandmothers and my peers saved us; we have female words—feminine, maiden, matron, and crone. My daughter and son have more freedom to cross the traditional lines of his and hers; we share tasks and professions.

5

The Rice Goddess **embellished**

Beautiful maidens slid down the rainbow to play in an earthy pond on Mount Kramat in Java. They took off their heavenly clothing and hung them on the bushes. They chattered and laughed, swam, danced, and ate heavenly nectar and rice.

Noticing the sun set, they jumped from the pool to put on their clothing. One Heavenly Maiden frantically looked everywhere for her clothes, lost. She pleaded with her friends, "Please stay while I find my clothing. The air is cold here. Please don't leave me all alone. I'm scared."

The others had to go or else trapped on earth. She sobbed; she moaned. "Please, please stay."

They left her hiding, scared. The maiden grabbed leaves to wrap around herself to keep warm. She saw a young man; he had a cloth full of wood on his back.

"Oh, please, dear lad, help me. My clothes are missing." As he approached, he seemed gentle, reliable, and concerned. "I live down this lane. I will ask my grandma for some clothes for a young maid stranded in these woods."

The Heavenly Maiden waited in the cold dark, frightened, wondering what was to become of her. She wailed, cuddling in dry leaves for warmth. Coming up the lane, she recognized the young man. He brought his grandma.

"What is a young maiden doing here?"

Hiding who she was and that she came from the heavens to play with friends in the pool, the maiden answered, "I came with friends from a village to bathe in the warm pool."

Grandma handed the Heavenly Maiden peasant clothing. She knew and glared at her grandson, saying, "Can we take you to your village?"

"I do not know where. I followed my friends." The maiden looked down and started to weep.

"You may come back to our village and may stay with me until my son finds your village."

Of course, the young man searched; of course, he found nothing.

The Heavenly Maiden went to the pool repeatedly, hunting for her clothing, finding nothing, only a few grains of the heavenly rice around the pond. She cleaned the grains carefully and wrapped them in cloth for the time she needed them.

With years passing, the young maiden remained in the village, learning the ways of the villagers. She had nowhere to go, so the Heavenly Maiden decided to marry the youth, who helped her. The celebration was simple—she had no family and no wealth. She lived in his hut and received a pot as a gift to fix their meals.

When alone, while her husband worked in a garden growing vegetables, she unwrapped the precious grains of heavenly rice. She laid the fire, poured water into the pot. When the water boiled, the sacred savory grains swelled, ready to eat. The maiden always saved a handful for the next meal. Once served and grains eaten, she washed the pot and put the saved grains rice inside.

Of course, her husband became curious, "Why does this pot always cook the delicious grains?"

"Please, husband, do not look into my cooking pot."

Of course, he looked and saw a handful of gains.

The maiden poured water to boil the handful of rice. When she opened the pot, the grains remained the handful, not full. Her husband looked, her magic gone.

Stuck without food, she had four lovely children to tend, a house, a husband. She took the remaining grains of rice and planted them in the shallow pond by the hut. As the grains sprouted and grew, she tended and weeded them. Soon they had flowers and then seeds. She harvested the few plants. She replanted many grain and cooked the rest for her starving family.

She toiled for years, becoming old and frail, ready to die. Still, she labored over the rice. Her children and neighbors helped. One night at dinner with her children at the table, her husband admitted, "I looked into the pot." She said nothing and looked down at the table and around at bowls of rice. Her husband admitted, "I hid your clothes."

Standing, she glared into his eyes, "You, you have no honor." She went outside, looking into the sky.

Her husband came outside. Reaching under the hut, he took a basket and gave the basket to her. Carefully, she unwrapped her clothing, as her children watched.

"All these years, a lie, a deception! WHY?"

"Wife, I found the jewels at the end of the rainbow dancing in the warm pool. I wanted a maiden as mine. I took the clothing and waited. You, dear wife, came to me."

Looking at her husband, then at her children, she yelled, "I'm returning home."

Her deceitful husband sank to his knees, consumed with shame. The Heavenly Maiden put on her clothing, becoming young again. She grabbed her children and disappeared.

For years, she looked from Heaven at her husband suffering alone and shamed. The neighbors ignored him and did not speak to him. They built a shrine to her, the Heavenly Maiden, who gave the stable for their life—rice.

After years of seeing his anguish, hurt, loss, and suffering, she forgave him, and at the full moon, returned with her children to visit until he left this earth.

✦✦✦✦✦✦✦

Why labor is a gift?

Usually, receiving rewards are an honor. Unfortunately, these folktales from the male's perspective speak of "females as mysterious." Females wanted and used for the gifts they bring. A helplessly abandoned "a damsel in distress" stripped of her identity, depending on a young lad for help; all the while, he is the deceiver. The captured maiden offered her gifts to the male within his society's norms and codes. She accepted these without question giving her talents to the man that stole her. I think of the secretaries who did all the work in the office, and the male boss got the credit. Many of my peers did this for "him."

Even when I attended university, the females educated for the service trades…to become nurses or teachers. I had two female professors, one in English and another in Biology. Other courses—law, science, economics, and music, even the arts— taught by male professors, while the female professors taught the serving trades.

Today, females are still treated as second class. I sign second on documents, and my husband is listed first on bills and bank accounts.

✦✦✦✦✦✦

The Heavenly Maiden is honored in every kitchen of Java, a satisfying ending for another damsel, a woman server. However, this tale later twisted by the male royalty—the Heavenly Maiden fed her daughter in a secret hut built by her husband. Then this daughter married a king; thus, she became royalty to suit his spread of his prestige—his relationship to the Rice Goddess honored.

✦✦✦✦✦✦

For egos this tale is told around the world in different versions, always from his point of view. Something from a maiden stolen is a theme in folktales: in Greek myths, the peeping tom, Ireland the Selkie, the Nordic stories of stolen skin, China stolen wings, and today in traditional tales with the male voice. "He" steals of our narratives.

Remember, giving is the feminine part of all of us, male and female. Do not let others take our gift for their profit at our loss. The wholeness of the contribution must be recognized as worth, not damaged by foolish greed to possess either gender's worth and pride.

Elisa and the Eleven Swans **modified**

Princess Elisa had all the love she needed only her happiness did not last. Her mother died. Elisa cried and cried for her. Soon afterward, her father married a wicked stepmother. A week later, a banished Elisa forced to live with poor peasants by the evil stepmother. Then, she changed Elisa's eleven brothers into voiceless swans.

The eleven swans passed over the cottage where Elisa lived. They hovered over the roof, flapping their wings. She did not see them; she did not hear their muted cries. Elisa remained at the peasant cottage alone, weaving, remembering the friendship and love from her brothers.

Elisa grew more beautiful each day. When she turned fifteen, her father sent a carriage for her. The wicked stepmother, mad with jealousy, met Elisa on the stairs. With the maids helping, she held Elisa down smearing walnut stain over her face and arms, rubbing oil and dirt into her hair, and tearing her dressed in rags.

Elisa yelled, "Where are my brothers?"

The evil stepmother sneered, "They are not here to help. Long ago, I turned them into swans."

Taken to her father, he yelled, "This is not my daughter, Elisa. This filth and ugliness is someone else."

Elisa ran from the castle. Longing for her mother, she ran until she reached a forest. She decided to find her eleven brothers. While she sobbed, night fell into darkness; the woods became silent. Elisa sat against a tree waiting for morning and fell asleep.

Then she woke to sounds of splashing water. Making her way to the spring, she dipped her hands into the rushing water. In a reflection, Elisa saw her ugly face, and rubbed off the stains. She then washed her hair and torn dress.

By the stream, an old crone sat with a basket of berries. She offered Elisa red and blue berries to eat.

"Kind lady, have you seen eleven princes with golden crowns?"

"Yesterday, eleven swans with gold crowns on their heads swam near the river by the ocean." The old crone led Elisa down the hill to the river, which she followed to the ocean. Scattered on the shore, caught in the seaweed, were eleven swan feathers.

At sunset, Elisa saw eleven swans with golden crowns on their heads fly to the shore. Flapping their long white wings, the swans settled. As the light sank below the water, the swan's feathers disappeared, and Elisa saw eleven handsome men. She ran, calling their names. Between laughter and tears, they talked of the wicked stepmother, who spun the horrid spell.

"I shall free you, my brothers."

"We fly away tomorrow and cannot return for a whole year."

"Please take me with you." "Dear sister, we will."

The brothers spent the night knotting a net from willow branches. Elisa snuggled on the net and fell asleep. With their beaks, the eleven swans picked up the net and flew high into the clouds when the sun rose.

All day, they flew through the sky above the ocean. Elisa looked down and saw the massive waves. That evening, she watched a storm blow towards them from the edge of the ocean. Furiously, the swans flew faster. Dark clouds thickened, as lightning struck the water.

Quickly, the swans darted down; Elisa thought she fell.

As the sun sank beneath the waters, the swans hovered. Elisa saw a rock. Then, her feet touched the solid stone. As the light darkened, her eleven brothers stood arm in arm around Elisa. The ocean splashed and pounded against them. Elisa, with her brothers, sang songs and told of their happy family.

When the morning light rose above the ocean, the swans flew up with Elisa. While the sun blazed in the sky, Elisa watched the giant waves. By evening, Elisa saw blue hills, then cedar forests, and towns with palaces. As sunlight disappeared, Elisa stood on a hill in front of a cave covered with green vines. Her brothers showed her where to sleep.

"Goodnight, brothers, I will find a way to help you."

In a dream, Elisa met the fairy Morgana, who told her, "You have the power to free your brothers. You have courage and determination. Do you see the nettles growing outside this cave? The nettles also grow in church-yards. Gather them, smash them with your bare feet, and break them into stocks. Knit the stocks into eleven shirts with wide, long sleeves. Throw the shirts over the eleven swans. The spell will break. Remember, from the moment you start until you finish, never speak a word, or pain will strike your brothers' hearts and cause their deaths."

In the light of the morning, Elisa saw the nettles. She picked the weeds, which burned large blisters on her fingers. Elisa smashed the nettles with her bare feet, as burning blisters flared on them. She cared nothing of pain, her concern only to release her brothers from the spell. Elisa worked without rest while her brothers, the swans, swam on a lake.

One day, a hunting horn rang out among the trees. The swans flew into the sky, Elias fled into her cave with a hound following, pacing back and forth and howling. A young king entered.

"How did you come here, fair maiden?"

Elisa shook her head; she dare not speak.

"Come with me."

Elisa wept and pointed to the shirts and nettles.

"I only want to make you happy; you will thank me one day."

The young king took Elisa to his palace. She let the maids wash and dress her in a royal gown and weave pearls into her hair, then pull long soft gloves over her blistered fingers. Her beauty overpowering.

In a little room, Elisa lived. On the walls hung green-leafed tapestries, which resembled vines on the cave. She had velvet and silk as her bed. On the floor were her bundles of nettles, and the shirts hung on the wall. Elisa bowed her head in respect; she dare not speak.

She grew fonder of the young king every day. Only she remained silent until she finished the shirts. Her brothers must be men night and day.

On knitting the seventh shirt, Elisa ran out of nettle stocks. She crept down the stairs into the moonlit garden, walked through closed markets until she reached the graveyard. On a new tomb sat ugly ghouls. They dipped their long bony fingers into the grave and ate the dead. Elisa passed behind them, gathered the stinging nettles, and carried the weeds back to the castle.

One day, the king came and asked, "Dearest maiden, will you marry me and be the queen of my land?" Elisa kissed the king's hand. He hugged her.

"My silent maiden is to be my queen. I ring the bells of the kingdom, to announce our wedding."

While knitting the eleventh shirt, Elisa again ran out of nettles, one last trip through the horrid ghouls in the graveyard. As she left the palace, a guard followed her. As ghouls ate the dead, the guard turned away. He did not see Elisa slip around the horrid.

As Elisa walked back to the palace, the guard snatched her and dragged her to a dark cell. The nettles tossed on the floor, and the ten shirts hurled around the room. Elisa knitted the eleventh shirt during the night.

The next morning, Elisa rode to her death. Ten shirts were beside her. She continued to knit the eleventh shirt.

Villagers followed the cart, poking and mocking, "Take those shirts away. She does demon's work."

High in the sky, the eleven swans found Elisa. They flew to the cart, perched on the edges, and flapped their broad white wings. The people drew back. Elisa threw the eleven shirts over each swan.

The spell broken, each swan turned into a handsome man. One brother's arm remained a wing because Elisa had not woven the last sleeve for the eleventh shirt. Then Elisa and her brothers traveled back to their father's kingdom to settle with the wicked stepmother.

⸻ ✦✦✦ ⸻

Why remain loyal to goals?

This tale shows that acceptance without fighting, screaming, or anger works for the family to maintain loyal to each other. This story says accept, be patient, work diligently on your goal, and you will liberate your family and yourself.

I was not a princess needing to save eleven brothers. I interrupted the tale to break my curse, fight the traditional social norm that stated to marry at eighteen, and still remain loyal and hold respect for the family. I wanted an education to expand my life and still be respected by my family, maybe more respect.

This tale warned me to stick with my goals, finish that education, no matter the hindrances. As Elisa worked, during my time and place, I worked to break the curse of the struggling working class: "All life is a struggle." This barrier is a norm for the wealthy male social class.

An education brought me choices. Working for my purpose was worth all the obstacles encountered; I am now a writer, artist, and storyteller and loyal to my primary and secondary families.

Notes about Elisa

How can a wicked woman destroy everything without a man's awareness? "Never trust the other woman," floats through my mind. Like the Grimm Brothers and Lang's stories always a wicked stepmother full of jealousy runs the life of the fat**her** and ruins the other wo**man's** children, in this tale the eleven sons, especially the daughter. (Note the word **her** included in the spelling of fat**her** and for mot**her** and brot**hers**.) I always wondered, "Where is the father?" while a wicked wo**man** ruins "his" family. (Note the word **man** included in the spelling.)

Or…is this tale about politics of the time, the norms to direct the lives of every person: the wicked stepmother (ruler), wealthy father (advantage), daughter (to work and serve), and the eleven brothers (trapped by rules)?

⁑⁂⁑

This folktale gives credit to Hans Christian Anderson for writing. After reading his effort to write creative stories, as all excellent storytellers, he followed the traditional folktale plot and added the beauty of the sea, roses, and the swan. I figured Hans added parts of stories together that servants told while making rugs and cloth or laborers knotting nets for fish to spinning tales of hope. Enhanced folklore from the sailing community Hans Christian Anderson wrote for the royal courts thus given credit for the folk stories.

The gooseneck is a tool used for a third hand while netting, an interesting motivation for a story.

7

Enid's Narrative adapted from Geraint, Son of Erdin

My name is Lady Enid; my father is Lord Earl Ynywl of Laluth. This is my story about my Knight Geraint and his last quest.

On horseback, Geraint and I rode for three days. We came to a castle on a hill by the ocean. We rode through the gates and inside, greeted with cheers. The guards took us to King Arthur and Lady Gwenhwyvar, who waited in the hall.

Geraint asked, "Did Knight Edeyrn, Son of Nudd, give his apology?"

Lady Gwenhwyvar answered, "He traveled wounded and apologized, stating his defeat to you and that he is in service to Knight Geraint."

The apology pleased Geraint.

Knight Edeyrn is why I am with Geraint in King Arthur's Court. Geraint followed Knight Edeyrn, his lady, and the dwarf into a village. When I saw the handsome youth, I sighed, "If only I was his maiden."

The youth came to our castle and asked for lodging. Geraint said he come to avenge Lady Gwenhwyvar, who the Knight's dwarf insulted. Bluntly, he asked my father if I might be his maiden and his wife. I accepted with a smile.

The Geraint needed armor and, again, bluntly asked my father, who was more than willing to have a knight as a son-in-law.

I rode with Geraint to the conquest of the Sparrow Hawk, where he challenged the Knight Ederyn. After a long battle with lances and swords, with my father's sharpest lance, Geraint injured Ederyn, who though wounded, had to journey to Lady Gwenhwyvar and apologize. Then Geraint told my cousin, Earl of Luluth, who stole our property, to return the castle and lands to my father, with all debts owed to my father paid.

While Geraint talked to Sir Arthur, I followed Lady Gwenhwyvar to her chambers. She chose for me garments of the most elegant linens and my wedding gown.

When Geraint and I married, foods, music, dancing, plays, storytelling, and mounds of gifts served to the guests…feasting in the court for days. The head of the White Stag presented to me the fairest of the ladies at Sir Arthur's Court.

Geraint played in the tournaments and gained much fame, honor, praise, and power. We were wealthy with the jewels he won.

Some months later, a messenger arrived in Sir Arthur's court from Geraint's father, Sir Lord Earl of Cornwall, who was uncle to King Arthur. My Geraint and Sir Arthur were cousins.

The note stated, "Sir Erbin wanted Geraint his son to stop playing in tournaments and defend the boundaries of their land. Sir Lord Earl Erbin showed poor health and neighbors are challenging his rights to boundaries."

Geraint refused, wanting to stay with Sir Arthur, who advised Geraint to visit his father with his lovely lady.

We traveled to the Castle of Sir Lord Earl Erbin and his lady. We had an assembly of twenty knights, including Knight Edeyrn; a judge; and gifts for Lord Erbin, the nobles, and people.

After our gifts, the feasting and games for our assembly began.

Geraint's mother and father received me with kindness. Geraint and I lodged in Geraint's front bedroom with the finest of furnishings. Knight Edeyrn and his lady stayed as visitors; the other knights slept in the field with foods prepared for them and tents for sleeping.

Sir Lord Erbin called a meeting of his nobles and asked them to give homage to his son Geraint as their king.

Geraint said, "I am not ready to be king."

He continued his challenges in games and tournaments to build his prestige. We had a lovely time.

One day, Geraint's father, Sir Lord Erbin, came to me and asked for my council. "Geraint is not his manly self, challenging in many tournaments, and has lost power for his father. The boundaries of our kingdom need protection."

That night I sobbed. "Geraint, I keep you from duties to the boundaries of your father's kingdom. You lose your warlike frame; your courage disappears." Looking at him, I cried.

Geraint looked at me with wild eyes; he raged with anger. "Do you want me to challenge my death? Or wish for another society? You shall have both."

Geraint ordered our horses brought. We visited his father, "Keep our possession for our return."

In our room, Geraint ordered, "Wear your oldest riding clothes." I did; then, I helped Geraint put on his armor and armored his horse. He took all his swords and lances. Our saddles completely stuffed with dried venison and fruits.

"Be silent, never talk to me, and stay far way in front. I will hold back. Remember, Enid, never talk to me."

We rode through tangled gnarled trees in the woods filled with wild beasts and thieves; I rode in front of Geraint. I was frightened and unsure what my husband, Knight Geraint, intended.

I rode in front quietly; so quiet I could hear the birds and the tramping of the horses. As I rode forward, the birds stopped singing. Four robbers watched from the hill, planning the murder of Geraint, then my capture and my undoing. I rode back to Geraint.

"Lady, I asked you to be quiet."

"Up the trail, four men wait!"

The four robbers charged toward Geraint, who had his lance up, stabbing and poking them. He took his sword out and whacked, knocking them off their horses one at a time. Then Geraint sliced off their heads and left the bodies bleeding on the ground. He took their armor and helmets, tied them together, and secured the armor on each horse. I was horrified—four men just like that, dead.

He said, "Now watch these four horses. Go up ahead of me. Don't talk to me. Don't say anything. I am riding behind."

I thought, "Oh, my god, so this is the quest I'm traveling."

I trotted ahead. Everything went well. Then I heard three robbers say, "They are going to take the knight to do with me what they wanted."

I rode back to Geraint to warn him, "Look, three warriors come."

The robbers galloped down the path, charging.

He said, "Enid..." Before he could finish, the robbers rushed him. With his lance, Geraint knocked them off their horses. Geraint dismounted and did as before, cut off their heads one at a time. My god, I never witnessed people killed. Again, he took the helmets and armor from the dead bodies and tied them to their horses. "Enid, don't worry, animals will eat them, or people will bury them." I got sick. Geraint was vile and unaffected.

"Enid, you will be the death of us. Stay quiet and lead with these seven horses. Do not talk to me."

I got my horse and trotted along the rocky path. Well, suddenly, five robbers came my way. I got scared, turned, and rode with the horses and armor down the trail. I did not care if Geraint was to kill me. He must know.

Before I knew, five warriors were crashing on Geraint, who had his lance out, knocking them off their horses. I couldn't see the battle, which was too fast. Then he jumped from his horse and chopped off their heads. Before, I knew he had their helmets and their armor removed, and he stacked them on the five horses.

"Enid, take these twelve horses and ride to the trees; we will stay there. No talking the whole night! You will feed and guard the horse while I sleep. Stay awake until morning."

Geraint walked his horse over to the trees, dismounted. With his armor on, he leaned against the tree and fell asleep. I was awake the whole night. Strange sounds frightened the horses, which moved back and forth. "Is this craze quest, is this the society of which Geraint talked?" I wondered.

I did not wake Geraint in the morning. Who would he be when awake? Finally, he said, "Okay, get on your horse, lead the twelve horses. I'm behind."

We came out of the trees into fields of crops, which mowers cut. We trotted along the river, and the mowers waved at us. When we stopped by the river, they watched us drink and water the horses. A youth walked to us with breakfast from the mowers, who waved again.

We ate bread, dried meats, and cheese, and drank wine. Geraint, happily, said, "I cleaned the country of the robbers." I had no realization of this happening. I only saw battles and dead bodies. "So, this what my knight does?"

Geraint asked the youth, "Where is lodging?"

"I will take you."

"Take us to the best inn, and we will spend the night."

At the inn, the innkeeper respectfully greeted us. Geraint requested, "Fix the best fest possible." To the youth, Geraint directed, "Buy and take foods to the mowers." He also said to the sprite. "You can be my paige. I'm going to give you the best horse, that is yours to keep."

"I can't take the horse, is too much."

"You will earn the horse with the harness. Go from door to door and tell everyone to come to a feast at the inn tomorrow evening...especially, invite the Earl Drwm."

We entered the inn and ate, then climbed upstairs to wash and sleep. Later in the evening, we walked downstairs into the feast and music.

Geraint said, "You speak with the maiden and ladies. I will tend the men and the knights with foods and drinks."

While I chatted with the women, an ominous, dark, heavy man stared at me. Earl Drwm came over to me. "Tonight, I will kill your knight. Then, I'm going to take you. I'm going to do what I please to you and cast you away if you don't cooperate."

"You threaten to kill my knight?"

"Yes, I do. My twelve knights will help."

I thought better to have Geraint away from Earl Drwm; the inn belonged to him. I playfully answered, "Why don't we meet in the morning, here."

After everyone left, Geraint and I quietly went up to bed. I let him sleep for a while. Then I lit a candle and awoke him. "The Earl Drwm said he is to kill you. He will take me and do what he wants and cast me off."

Geraint became so angry, his face went white, then across that expression came horror. "You did well. Get your clothes."

I helped Geraint put on his armor.

Geraint informed the innkeeper, "We needed our horses. Oh, you can have the eleven horses with the armor attached. Please, you can use the money."

The innkeeper accepted the eleven horses, "Thank you, I will buy the inn."

"Which way is out of town?" He directed us to ride beside the fields to the side of the trees.

Riding on the trail, we heard horses galloping—Earl Drwm chased us. We rode into a field, followed by Drwm with his twelve knights.

We stopped in a clearing. The knights circled Geraint; the weakest dared the first to challenge.

One by one, Geraint dismounted the knights with spears until he injured the twelve. The Earl Drwm remained. Drwm was weakened with one whack from Geraint's sword; he dropped, begging, "*mercy!*"

"Take care of your men. Leave here; do not return." Geraint let him go, not killing the Lord.

Saddling, we rode on and rode on. Then, all of a sudden, we round a hill. I saw a delightful castle in the most beautiful country I had seen.

A knight approached Geraint. "No, this is not the trail; the King Frank owns the land. Take the lower trail."

"I will not," said Geraint.

"Nobody goes up there. You have to go down this way. King Gwiffer Pieti will slay you."

Behold, I saw the king down in the field. He rode a massive horse with the shiniest armor. The smallest king I had seen.

Geraint continued, "I'm taking the road into the village."

"No, no, no! That belongs to Frank King Gwiffer Pieti. He'll be here."

Galloping towards us appeared the king ready for battle.

Geraint and the King clashed and banged their lances. Finally, Geraint knocked the king off his horse. Heedless, Geraint dismounted; the king rushed and struck his sword through Geraint's helmet to his left shoulder.

Enraged, Geraint, with one swing of his sword, glazed the king's helmet, splitting the skull of the small king.

Falling on his knees, "*merci!*" begged the small king.

Geraint laughed, "My king, you will be my ally and come if I need help."

Gwiffer Pieti pleaded with Geraint, "Come and heal your wounds in my castle."

"No, I have more quests to make."

Among the trees, away from the sun, we rested. I was exhausted; Geraint, hot, and his blood covered his armor.

Up rode a paige, and minutes later, a squire with armor and a lance.

The squire asked, "What are you doing, old man?"

"I'm resting from the sun."

The squire rushed at Geraint with his lance. Geraint knocked him off his horse and laughed.

"You are Squire Kia."

Next, a steward on his horse headed for Geraint, who knocked him off his horse and laughed, "You are Steward Gwalshmai."

"Geraint, this is you. Sir Arthur is on the trail; come and join us."

"No! I'm tired, dirty, hungry, and very stressed. I will rest on the trail."

I said, "Knight Geraint does not think about his wound."

I heard the steward tell the paige, "Have Sir Arthur pitch his tent by the road. Tell them Geraint is found and wounded."

Steward Gwalshmai helped Geraint on his horse in a pretense to ride with us down the trail.

We arrived at the camp of Sir Arthur, who insisted, "Geraint, get off your horse and come to the tent for healing."

"No!" "Yes?" "No?" Finally, after a fall from his horse, "Yes!"

Geraint hasty carried to the doctor's tent. For a month, herbs and oils applied to his wounds.

"I refresh in Lady Gwenhwyvar's tent, enjoying foods, bathing, and chatting."

After that month, when Geraint's wound healed, we traveled down the road again. On the quest again and not far down the road, we heard a lady wailing and screaming.

We came upon a knight beaten and clubbed. The lady said, "Three giants came down the road, battled, and killed my knight. They walked up the hill with his armor and horse."

Geraint said, "I will follow their trail to take revenge."

I waited with the lady for hours.

Finally, Geraint came out from the trees, his left shoulder again smashed. With the dead knight's armor as before, Geraint tied on the knight's horse. Geraint fell off his horse; I tended his wound while he spoke about the battle.

"I rode up the hill and spotted the three giants walking in the valley. I dismounted my horse and tied him to a tree to follow the three. I came behind them, yelling. They turned; we battled with swords. I had the three giants knocked down and beheaded before they knew. I took the stolen horse and armor and walked back to my horse, not knowing I was wounded."

Geraint passed out and left the lady and me alone. I had enough and screamed. Along the road came several knights, whose leader introduced himself as Earl Limoris.

They buried the dead knight. The other lady and I mounted our horses, and Geraint placed on his shield to drag him to Earl Limoris' castle.

At the castle of Earl Limoris, his servants spread a feast for the lady and me.

"Here are new garments to wear."

"I only wear what my knight chooses."

"Here, eat this food."

"I will not eat until my knight eats."

"Here, drink this liquor to help you obey me."

"I only drink with my knight."

With that last answer, the Earl Limoris hit my ear. I screamed. Geraint jumped off the shield and ran his sword through the earl's neck. His court and servants ran out of the castle, yelling. "A ghost killed the earl."

Geraint gave the lady the castle and boundaries.

Although dark, we left the castle; we found our horses and rode up the trail. As our horses trotted along, we heard hoofs beating the ground behind us. Geraint slid off his steed and braced his lance for an attack.

The Frank King Gwiffer Peiti said, "Geraint, I've come to help."

At King Gwiffer Peiti's Barron's castle, Geraint again rested a month with oils and herbs applied to his shoulder. The castle and yards were as lovely as the ladies. I had an excellent time. When Geraint healed, he said, "I must go; I have one more quest to finish."

As we trotted through the hedges with Gwiffer Peiti, a knight met us. "Do not go into the mist; you will lose your life."

Geraint galloped down the trail to the mist. We followed the knight.

I prayed, "Oh, dearest spirits, let this pass from us."

Lord Earl Owain, who owned the hedge and the mist enchantment, stopped Geraint from traveling farther and invited us to dine with him.

Inside tents, Gwiffer Peiti and I ate with the Earl Owain.

Geraint would not eat, insisting. "I must go into the mist."

Earl Owain agreed. "As you insist on your death, you may."

"Where do I go?"

"Where you are taken."

"What do I ask?"

"That there is an end."

Into the mist, Geraint rode with his readied lance. In seconds, we heard a horn; Geraint appeared, smiling!

He told of his adventure, his last quest:

In the Hedge of Mist, I followed a trail through a maze. Stuck in the hedge were slain knights' heads mounted on poles, some skeletons and others with flesh. Finally, I rode into a meadow. In the distance, I saw a red silk tent and a single apple tree. I trotted over and dismounted. I tied my mount to the tree and ventured inside. The White Maiden with golden hair sat in a gold chair. "This chair belongs to the Black Knight."

I found myself outside, riding with lance in hand against the Black Knight. Stabled, I fell off my horse. The knight challenged with his sword. We battled until I slashed the knight through his helmet.

The Black Knight begged, "*mercy*! What can I do for you?"

I asked, "How do I stop the enchantment of the games?"

The knight answered, "Blow the horn on the apple tree."

Here I am, that quest was easy.

Earl Owain laughed and offered a toast to Geraint for his bravery.

We stayed with Earl Owain to rest, then said good-bye to King Gwiffer Peiti and traveled to Geraint's father.

At the Castle in Cornwall, his father, Sir Lord Erbin, greeted us, delighted and satisfied with his son. He heard of Geraint's trumpets and the expanded boundaries for the kingdom. His father and the court crowned Geraint as King of Cornwall, and Geraint also became a Knight of Sir Arthur's Round Table.

From then on, I lived comfortably and in peace with my king and Knight Geraint.

◆◆◆◆◆

Why praise the Knight in Shining Armor?

Enid, a wise woman, uses esteem for her husband's successes and adoration for what he provides. Lady Enid "stands by her man," her Knight Geraint, an irresponsible husband, a warrior, who takes Lady Enid on a long endangered, perilous journey. With his helmet on his head, sword in hand, the spear and lance ready to win, and his lady by his side as a prize. The armored warrior is on his quest. Enid travels with him, horrified and astonished, and marvels at her husband's compelling drive. He is to prove he is a grand warrior, her Knight in Shining Armor, worthy of her admiration beyond his conquests in tournaments.

＋＋◆＋＋

In my teenage years, the armor was the hopped-up car, which was fast and growled. The macho male built and prowled in this car to prove himself, showing off and drag racing on the streets. The cars were shiny works of art, like a knight's armor. And the macho male had a beautiful lady sitting close to him and her arm around him, both proud. My brother was this male and had his shining armor.

I understand the burdens around the armored code placed on young lads who struggle to win as warriors. The "Knight in Shining Armor" is a curse to both sexes. The desire to be part of that energy was more than I could manage.

My brother, a car man, drove his armor; the narrative suited him. I loved my brother, who, after Covid-19, with all his aliments, took his life. Only a Knight in Shining Armor has this amount of courage.

Notes about Lady Enid's Narrative

The legend is part of the ancient verbal Mabinogion Myth from the early the fourth century or before. Various versions crossed between Wales and France, Brittany, with a bit of Germanic influence. Stories spread with the traders and the troubadours, who rode along the trading routes.

＋＋◆＋＋

This lengthy tale, *Geraint, Son of Erbin* from the *Welsh Mabinogion*, the primitive Celtic Arthurian Myths was translated into English in 1849 by Welch Lady Charlotte Guest. My version is depicted in scenes to help listeners or readers with the battles. I adapted, cut, and modified the long epic journey into simple English in the third person and past tense to focus the telling for today's audiences. The narrative is told from Lady Enid's Daughter of Earl Ynywl, which was never told orally or written in a female narrative in classic tales.

8

Innocent Red embroidered from *Little Red Riding Hood*

Once upon a time, in a land far away, or not so far away, lived Innocent Red, who readies for her day's journey to Granny's house. She dresses in her new red hooded cape, picks up her basket of goodies for Granny, and flings her pack on her back. This pack has her tools and skills and room for more.

Innocent Red opens the door and steps onto the porch. As she walks across the porch, a pack of wolves sneaks along the side. Twigs and leaves on the ground rustle and snap.

Her dogs yap, *"Protection, protection, protection!"*

Innocent Red opens the gate, birds chirp, *"Beware, beware, be safe, be safe, watch, watch!"*

When she walks across the bridge that goes over a creek, her two cats follow, swishing their tails back and forth, meowing, *"careful, careful."* She pets the two, then steps onto the dirt path. The cats swish their tails and watch Innocent Red step on the path into her day.

The wolves pursue her from the bushes.

Crows yell, *"Watch out! Wolves, many wolves!"* Not listening, Innocent skips to Granny's house. The wolf family follows her.

While Innocent Red travels on the path, wolves whisper in the bushes and study her. Father Wolf chooses the youngest, most handsome of his cubs. "You will entice Innocent Red to have lunch with you. Then lead her into the wrong path into the forest, where we will go for the kill, our feast of dinner." Mother Wolf approves.

On a lane, surrounded by lovely trees and flowers, walks the most handsome wolf, who steps in front of Innocent Red. The wolf smiles the most welcoming, warm, and sincere greeting. "My maiden, would you like to have lunch with me at the finest cafe in these woods?"

Not sure of his intentions while liking his charm, Innocent Red answers, "Yes! I'm to be at Granny's much later in the day." She takes his arm, and he leads the way.

A lunch prepared with the most delicious tastes and most elegant display arrives from the wolves' kitchen. Soon, Innocent Red becomes disenchanted with the handsome wolf, who is almost too perfect, smiles too much, and has too much knowledge of cuisines. He gazes lustfully at her while talking of this taste and that smell. His voice is a slow monotonous song. Innocent Red had enough; she must, should, and will dismiss herself.

"Time to be on my way. The lunch was delicious." She leaves the young dandy eating by himself, savoring every mouthful.

Father Wolf is furious with his youngest son.

Innocent Red enjoys the flowers outside as she skips merrily on her path through the woods. She loved the warmth of the middle of the day.

Father Wolf observes Innocent Red's rapture with the flowers and sends her next son to trap her. Mother Wolf agrees this is a good plan.

An elegant, strong wolf stands among the flowers with his shovel and greets Innocent Red with a gentle smile. "Oh!" she exclaims, "I see you are the gardener."

"Yes, I will explain the different flowers as we walk along this path."

His teeth shine, his eyes gleam bright, and his ears wide for listening. Innocent Red, intrigued, walks along with him. He shows her the beautiful flowers, tells her their names, encourages her to pick one or two and cast seeds. He walks Innocent Red further and further from her path into the thickest, darkest forest. Innocent Red's head, alight with colors and fragrances, notices that the sun lowers into afternoon.

"I must, should, and will be on my way. So kind of you to show me the flowers; I will take these to my Granny." Swiftly, she traces her steps back along the thin dirt trail to her path. "That was a long way into the forest."

Father Wolf is furious and irritated with this son. Mother Wolf has another idea. "Daughter, dress in your finest perfume, jewelry, hat, and coat. Then, take Innocent Red shopping to tire her, then walk along the back path with the spiked high heels. We will come for our feast."

When Innocent Red sees the glamorous wolf, she is full of admiration. "You are quite stunning."

The wolf asks, "Would you like to shop with me? I'll show you the finest shoes and the best gloves."

"Sure, new shoes and maybe a pair of gloves to go with my new red cape."

At the fashion shop, the wolf and Innocent Red try on shoes after shoes and gloves after gloves. After a while, Innocent Red looks at the wolf, "Although the spiked high heels are lovely and the gloves fit marvelously, I see the sun approaches late afternoon. My Granny expects me. I must not, should not, and will not be late to her house." Innocent Red runs from the fashion shop.

Ready for the feast, then displeased, irritated, and furious with his daughter, Father Wolf sends the most dashing, viral killer of the pack, his oldest son. Mother Wolf agrees this son has the skills.

Innocent Red notices the handsome wolf with gorgeous eyes; smooth, shiny gray fur; lovely long ears; and the brightest of smiles. The wolf tips his hat to her and leans on his cane. He is a dandy—strong, viral, and cunning. "I see you skip. You must love to dance. I know where the music is exciting." Curious, Innocent Red smiles and answers, "Yes, I have time to walk to Granny's house."

The handsome, distinguished wolf walks Innocent Red into the Wolfterra, a luxury tavern, best on the path to Granny's. The music, lights, and dancing at first are splendid. Nervous, Innocent Red knows time runs late and says to the dashing wolf, "I must hurry on my way. My Granny expects me. I must not, should not, and will not be late." Admired by the many ladies, the wolf does not see Innocent Red leave.

Late evening, Father Wolf finds his oldest son in the limelight, dancing and drinking with female wolves. "Where is Innocent Red?" The young dandy looks around, "Oh, she must be at her Granny's."

Father Wolf, displeased, furious, and irritated, takes the vile son by the ear. "Collect our family and meet me at Granny's house." Father Wolf orders, "Wife, go to Granny's house and capture her ready for eating."

Innocent Red takes her time, enjoying the colors in the evening sky as she talks to the happy walkers along the path. She does not notice large, Mother Wolf slip through the bushes along the path.

Granny is in her garden weeding when Mother Wolf arrives. The wolf sneaks through the front door and goes to Granny's bedroom. She dresses in Granny's nightgown and hat and waits on the bed. Granny enters the kitchen and starts the pot of water to boil for tea. Hearing a noise, she investigates and discovers a wolf in her bed.

Granny runs out the front door, into the forest, screaming. "Wolf! Wolf in my house." She searches for her husband, the woodcutter.

In the meantime, Innocent Red arrives at Granny's house. Granny is not in her garden, and her grandpa is not in his woodshed or in the orchard. So, Innocent Red goes inside and notices the water boiling in the kettle. She pours the hot water into the teapot, adds the tea, and places her cookies on a tray.

A grumble comes from the bedroom. Innocent Red enters the bedroom. On the bed lays a strange, sickly looking Granny. As trusting as she is naïve, Innocent Red walks over to Mother Wolf, who is wearing Granny's nightcap and nightgown.

"Granny, do you feel well?"

The wolf grumbles.

"Granny, what big eyes!"

The wolf growls, "Better to see you."

"Granny, what big ears!"

The wolf growls, "Better to hear you."

"Granny, what big sharp teeth you have!"

Mother Wolf opens her mouth wide and howls, "Better to eat you!"

With that howl, the wolf family rushes into the house to surround Innocent Red. Their eyes glow desire; saliva drips from their sharp teeth. Slowly, they approach, growling. Innocent Red picks up her pack, hitting, pounding, smacking, and knocking the wolves while shouting, "Where is my Granny?"

In the meantime, Granny finds Grandpa, and they run to the house. Grandpa readied to fling his ax. Before he can, the beaten wolves jump through the windows and push out the door.

The wolves run and hide deep in the forest, never to be seen again by Innocent Red, Granny, or Grandpa.

+ + + ◆ + + +

Why persist on your path?

What does the fifteenth century folktale say about Granny in *Little Red Riding Hood*? Is she that stupid to let a wolf eat her? Or, even worse, a wolf lives inside Granny. Horrors! No! I suspect a negative attitude about elderly women's capabilities.

+ + + ◆ + + +

Better to meet the wolves when young and beat them than eaten when elderly. Really! Hopefully, a youth, with the help of her Granny, the wood "would" cutter, and her pack of skills, will not be eaten or molested by a wolf. All along our paths, we will meet various wolves with many offerings to benefit their pleasures, not ours. Beware! Some wolves are disguised and with us for so long, they are hard to recognize.

After having my children and now being a grandmother and especially having a granddaughter and grandsons, I see the journey to Granny's house as a personal journey to stay on the path one selects to become elderly. A robust and positive protagonist, Old Granny, protects the child coming of age. Staying on my path, never deterred by social norms or intimidation, my young child saved my future, and I become what I desired. Now, Old Granny offers stories while having tea and cakes with her grandchildren.

Notes about Wolves

The wolf was the first tamed animal that helped the ancient hunters, and is now our pet dog. Wolves were vital to the forests, not to the people taking over the woods.

In the Middle-Ages, when farmers cut down the trees and took over the woods, wolves became evil, the monsters of horror stories, and villains of many disguises. The negative wolf is the enemy of man, the antagonist for many cautionary tales. I can imagine the wolf in survival mode wanting to eat men.

Today, the wolf is a metaphor. The bad wolf is an enemy who fools us for cunning purposes…eating of a sort, the theme of horror stories. Young children are not to talk to strangers because that person may be a wolf in a person's clothing, or, as in this folktale, dressed in Granny's clothing. A wolf is a damaging person we must avoid or manage for our safety.

9

Tatsuko, the Rainbow Dragon **enhanced**

A poor maiden Tatsuko wanted to be beautiful and live-forever. She helped her mother in the northern mountains of Japan a long, long time ago. The villagers admired Tatsuko; she worked hard and sang while they worked.

In the spring, Tatsuko liked to pick herbs from the mountains. She was the fastest rider on horseback. In the fields clearing the weeds, she helped start and watch the flames burn the weed, then planted seeds of hemp for later weaving. Tatsuko was durable and able. Her songs soothed everyone as they worked. Her voice was youthful and full of energy.

In the summer, Tatsuko's sweet voice rang like bells, calming the villagers' tired muscles while they chopped and stacked the hemp to dry. Then the hemp boiled in iron kettles with the fires burning day and night. Her hands were strong and agile, not twisted and crippled.

One hot and dry day, Tatsuko went to the spring to wash her face and hands. She noticed her reflection in the still water. Her face was young, not wrinkled or dry, alive. Tatsuko was as beautiful as her voice was clear and pleasing.

In the fall, she gathered and chopped hay for the horses to eat during the winter rains and snow. Tatsuko rode her horse like the wind and carried massive bundles of wood through the mountain passes. Her body was swift and quick, not bent and slow. She was as healthy and beautiful as her voice for singing.

In the winter, Tatsuko caught rabbits, skinned them for stew, and tanned their skin for coats and blankets. With the villages and her mother, she wove the hemp into straw mats for walls and floors. She carried on horseback the blankets, rugs, and mats to market to sell. She loved running in the snow; she was limber and fast. Her legs were strong, not crippled from age. In the hut during the evenings weaving with her mother, Tatsuko sang, staring into the fire, dreaming of a better life.

When work finished, Tatsuko walked to Goddess Benten in her temple to ask the Goddess to keep her young, agile, and healthy. Benten sat and listened. Once, when Tatsuko traveled during a blizzard, the Goddess spoke to Tatsuko's prayers, "You may have your wish, dear child. Do not share your wish with your mother and villagers. Drink the fresh spring waters."

After the long, cold winter, Tatsuko rode with maidens to gather herbs in the new flowering fields. While her friends took naps, Tatsuko searched for the spring of water as directed by the Goddess Benten. Finding the spring, Tatsuko cupped her hand, catching the water. As she drank, fire spit from the earth and a violent earthquake shook the valley.

Screaming and running into the valley, the frightened friends shouted, "Tatsuko is lost, gone." The villagers observed smoke swelling from the ground in the valley; they felt the earth shake.

"My daughter!" screamed Tatsuko's mother. She climbed through the burning trees with the villagers following. They walked over the upside down earth with rocks broken and displaced and burnt trees. A vast lake covered the valley. Everyone stood, shocked.

In the middle of the lake, a fountain sprayed with a rainbow reaching into the sky. From the burnt shores, Tatsuko's mother and the villagers watched a tiny, then huge, dragon approach the beach with the rainbow. The dragon stepped onto the beach. With bright, shining eyes and in a sweet singing voice, the dragon said. "I am Tatsuko."

As a maiden, Tatsuko appeared to her mother and hugged her.

"Why, Tatsuko?"

"When I went to the temple, I prayed to Goddess Benten, asking if I could be young and beautiful forever. Do you hear, forever! Not twisted with a bent body, no graying hair, no twisted fingers, and my voice clear, young."

"My daughter, work is my honor; my bent back is my pride. After your trips to the temple and nightly singing to Benten, then finally gathering herbs with your friends, I thought you were back with me."

"Mother, when I stared into the fire, I asked for beauty and youth. I went to the temple, those days through the snow and wind, to ask Benten to keep my face beautiful, my body spry, my hands youthful, and my hair shiny and black."

"Tatsuko, I need your help. Come back to me."

"Benten said that I could never go back, if I found the spring and drank its water. As I drank, my body got heavy, dizzy; I fainted. I have no regrets."

"Tatsuko, how could you want beauty over honor of work?"

"Mother, this is honor. I have wisdom. I sing all day."

"Tatsuko, my beautiful daughter, I have lost you."

"Mother, when you want fish to eat, I will hear and bring them."

Tatsuko backed into the lake. Turning, she became the Rainbow Dragon and swam away. Tatsuko's mother cried; as she cried, her tears turned into fish. Some of the fish followed the Rainbow Dragon; the rest stayed on the shore for the villagers.

◆◆◆◆◆

Why search for empowerment?

We can change our lives for our betterment. I can attest to this change. I grew up in a small working town of Colorado Springs with farming, mining, military, and factory work.

I did not want to become old and tired in a small backward town with a population of less than 30,000…nor married to a tired, overworked husband, having six children, while I worked in a factory for more income, or living alone, becoming a prostitute for money. I was college-bound; my grades were excellent. I received a scholarship and a National Defense

Loan. Education was offered to females and allowed into college from the more inferior parts of the U.S.

What is funny, in high school, in the school pictures for the yearbook for the clubs I was a member, and that was many. I wore a small crown in my hair. I did not care if my critical classmates noticed; they were into their own "thing." All these years, I wondered if my peers noticed when I wore a crown. I know why—I wore the crown; I moved beyond the small, petty prejudice. I owned my life; I was queen of myself.

At university, teaching was my choice… not many occupations for a mere girl. Most girls "found" their husbands.

After graduating, I flew to Alaska to teach. I left my family in Colorado, later settling in the Bay Area of California. Returning yearly with my husband and our children, we enjoyed the mountains and camping with my relatives. My mother and father visited, my brother twice, my grown nephews and niece once, and a now a niece lives near. I'm sure none of the villagers came to visit Tatsuko.

I did not affect change in my family; I became tolerant. I crossed norms and social lines, actually time traveling one hundred years ahead…physically moving from the standards and social enforcements of male domination. I released my family from the struggling norm; I could succeed.

Notes about Geishas

Tatsuko was beautiful, robust, and possibly more intelligent and more motivated than the other maidens in her impoverished Japanese village. Tatsuko's wish for a better life came true. Most young girls of my time wished for betterment in their lives. Tatsuko obtained her desire to have lasting beauty.

Tatsuko became a Geisha during the Edo period (1603–1867), the final period of traditional Japan, with internal peace, political stability, and economic growth under the Shogunate, the military dictatorship founded by Tokugawa Ieyasu. Educated in the arts—singing and playing instruments while serving tea to rich males—Tatsuko gained wealth and gave her mother fish, wealth.

When I told my friend Sarasa Tatsuko's story, she was overjoyed that anyone knew the Japanese story. Sarasa said her mother lives by the Lake

Tazawako. Later, the villagers did honor Tatsuko with a statue and that Tatsuko is still celebrated today as a legend.

Japanese Generals of the sixteenth century created a prosperous nation. The seventeenth century saw the rise of the city of Kyoto. Here, the rich had the fashion, courtesans, and eventually, the Geishas, who were educated in the arts: conversation, dance, music, literature, elegant calligraphy, and performing the tea ceremony. In the 1730s, both men and women were Geishas. They entertained like the jesters in the European courts. By the 1780s, Geishas were mostly women under strict governmental regulation. Geishas lived in Tea Houses, offering their fine arts, which supported the merchants: making gowns; Komodo; fans; hairdressing, wigs; makeup; and instruments for entertaining.

10

Sparrow's Gift adapted from *Tongue-Cut Sparrow*

Once, a long, long time ago, in a small Japanese village, an old sister adopted a little sparrow that she loved to feed each day. The sparrow played above her and her younger sister while they washed and starched kimonos for the wealthy villagers.

One day, old sister traveled into the forest to gather firewood to boil the starch pot. Younger sister was in the yard, putting the starch in the tub of water. The sparrow, the Komi spirit for the earth, sang to the younger sister.

"You good-for-nothing bird, I'll show you. You get food and water you don't deserve!" The younger sister grabbed her knife and threw it at the sparrow. The knife splashed into the tub of the starch, which spilled everywhere. To the innocent sparrow, the younger sister yelled, "Never return, I will cut your tongue out."

When older sister returned with the wood, no sparrow flew from the trees to greet her. "Sister!" called old sister, "Where is my sparrow?"

The younger sister replied, "Sparrow? That worthless bird drank all the starch for the washing tub, so I snipped its tongue. The bird flew away crying, *"Chun, Chun."*

"What a mean thing to do! I must go at once to apologize to the sparrow. She is a spirit of our earth." Leaving for the mountain, old sister wrapped her cloak around her for warmth and used her cane for balance. "Chun, Chun?" She called as she walked up the mountain path.

Soon she came to a man cleaning an ox. Old sister called, "Oxen washer, do you know the home of the sparrow?"

"Yes, the sparrows! Old sister, help me wash this ox and I will tell you."

Old sister scrubbed the ox with gentleness and kindness, especially careful around the ox's eyes and ears. She cleaned the ox's feet. The oxen washer, delighted, said. "Follow this path, you will come to a bamboo grove. There you will find the sparrow weaving in her garden."

Old sister bowed and climbed the path into the mountains, calling, "Chun, Chun!" The path was clean, well-tended, swept, flowers blooming, butterflies fluttering, bees buzzing, and birds singing. Old sister came into a tall bamboo grove. In the middle was a beautiful bamboo house. Many sparrows flew about singing. One sparrow wove on an enormous loom in a flower garden.

"Sparrow, oh sparrow!" called old sister.

When the sparrow heard old sister's voice, she flew to her, "Dear Grandmother, welcome to my humble home."

Old sister bowed, "My younger sister said she had snipped your tongue, I come with an apology."

The sparrow answered, "Your sister dumped over the starch, then cursed me. From you, no apology."

The sparrow gathered the other sparrows to meet the Grandmother. "Dine with us."

"I would like that," answered old sister.

Into the parlor they went. The sparrows generously served the old sister the whitest rice, the tastiest variety of sushi, and the freshest vegetables from the garden, and poured the most excellent green tea. "Please, enjoy our humble offering."

Old sister bowed her thanks to the sparrows. The sparrows delighted her with music and songs. The night was dark, so the sparrow invited, "Grandma, stay the night."

She rested on the most elegant bed of silks. During the night, which was on the full moon, old sister watched as the sparrows danced and sang.

Early the next morning, the sparrows gave old sister breakfast: fine green tea, miso soup, and rice. "We want to give you a gift to take home," offered the sparrows.

Old sister bowed, "You have done so much, I only came to apologize for my younger sister's dishonorable behavior."

The sparrow said, "We accept your apology and to honor that we offer our gift."

Placed on the floor were two wicker baskets, one large and the other small. "Please," encouraged the sparrow, "choose one, either the large one or the small one. Only, remember, Grandmother, you open the basket when you reach home."

Old sister bowed, "I am old, I will take the small one." The sparrows helped old sister put the small basket on her back, kept in place with her cloth wrap. "Good-bye, sweet sparrows please come again and sing at my home."

At the end of the bamboo grove, old sister bowed again to the sparrows. She walked down the mountain…the path smooth with an abundance of sweet smells from flowers, music from the insects and birds, and butterflies' folly.

The oxen washer bowed to old sister, "I thank you. The ox never felt better."

Old sister had the best walk, so pleasant and so refreshing; she was happy.

The old sister approached home; younger sister stopped her washing to scold, "Where have you been? I worried all night. How rude of you!"

"I apologized to the sparrow for your unkindness. They gave me dinner, the finest tea, sang songs, offered a fine bed of silk for sleeping, then offered breakfast in the morning, and as I left gave me a gift, this basket."

The younger demand, *"Open now, open!"*

Untying the cloth, the old sister gently slid the basket from her back and took the basket inside the house. She raised the lid. The basket fully packed with silver coins, beautiful silk cloth, a precious porcelain teapot with cups and teas, and still more beautiful gifts poured from the basket.

Younger sister became greedy, "Where is the sparrow?" Taking her wrap, she headed up the mountain. Old sister call after her, "Be gentle to the oxen and apologize to the sparrow in the garden."

"*Chun, Chun*!" Scoffed younger sister as she walked over a hard, rocky, rough path.

Younger sister came to the place where the oxen washer cleaned an ox. "Hey, washer! Where is the house of the sparrow?"

"House of the sparrow?" asked the oxen washer. "If you want to know, help me wash this ox."

"You heard what I said," shouted the younger sister. She took the brush with soap and smeared the dirty ox, getting soap in his eyes and ears. Then she threw cold water on him. "Done! Where does sparrow live?"

Hurrying on her way with no thank you or bow, younger sister hiked up a steep, gnarled path filled with sticking weeds and thorns. She tripped over rocks and roots. Finally, she entered the tall bamboo grove, which was so thick; she barely squeezed through. Birds flew about, squawking warnings. In the middle of the field of weed was a sparrow weaving.

"Hey!" bellowed younger sister.

"Yes, Grandmother, what honorable business may I help you with?"

"I come for the sparrow. I say again, louder, I've come for my old sister's sparrow."

A sparrow came from the humble hut with the other sparrows. The sparrow invited the younger sister inside—not into the parlor, but the kitchen porch. Put before the younger sister was millet gruel with grass soup and tea of sour weeds.

The younger sister sniffed and ate nothing. "Done! It's getting dark, show me my gift!"

"Yes," said the sparrow. "We shall give you one. But Grandmother, you must not open it until you are home."

The sparrows brought two wicker baskets, one big, the other tiny. "I'm strong and able," said younger sister, "I'll take that bigger one." She lifted the big basket onto her back, tying it with her wrap. She hurried from the sparrows' house without bowing and no apology for her behavior.

The basket became burdensome and more oppressive. The longer the young sister walked, the more exhausting the basket became. She thought, "The basket must hold many treasures." She sat down on the root of a tree to rest. Rain started pouring. She had to see; she untied the ropes, lifted the lid, and peeked. Something gleamed. "A bar of silver? Or a teapot of gold?"

The silver glint rose and coiled around the younger sister's arm. Horrified, she screamed! Other strange and horrid creatures flew from the basket and went for her. "Goblins!" Loud noise followed as she ran stumbling over rocks, tripping in the dirt, falling over roots, scratched by thorns with the goblins, ghouls, and ghosts chasing. Reaching home, younger sister pounded on the door. The goblins, ghouls, ghosts, toads, hornets, and hideous things swirled around and around the house. Old sister shouted from inside the house, "Apologize to the sparrows!"

Younger sister pounded and pounded, only met with silence. Finally, she shouted. "I apologize, sparrows!" Lamenting, she repeated over and over, "I apologize, sparrows!"

Old sister opened the door.

From that moment forward, younger sister gave water and seeds to the sparrows, remaining polite and quiet.

⋅⋅◆◆◆⋅⋅

Why value morality?

Shinto--the Komi, female energies is in all nature. Everything is alive; even rocks are to be honored and respected. All human beings of different origins, faiths, and sex are all equal as animals. Two old sisters show contrast in their travel and gifts given by sparrows, the Tarii spirits. Old sister honors and respects the sparrows she feeds and gives kind care to them as she gave to the ox she washed. For her decency and respect, she receives a reward. The greedy, demanding younger sister a basket of trouble she earned.

⋅⋅◆◆◆⋅⋅

Throughout our lives, we have many moral decisions to make. Unfortunately, rude and greedy is how people treat others when in offices, even in homes, especially in government and business. I observed this greed working in a small shop. One person who needs to be on top, sets the rules, and pecks the other workers as chickens caged in a coop, keeping other hens at the bottom.

In our society today, social laws detail the power structure. Married women sign below the husband's signature on documents, or where the male's name remains first on the checks, or, as my mother had a hell of a time closing accounts because Dad's name was on the bills. Women suppressed as servers in the second class; rich males owning money are of the first class. (My grandmothers from the farm with little education went with the standards, everyone becoming "better off.") My mother's generation protested norms; our generation's battled restraints and opened a few doors; our daughters recognized and have more equality. Pushed enough, stifled feminists fight social norms that alienate and hinder progress.

The shame is Asian, African, and Mexican cultures now excluded by social norms, standards, roles, and rules used to place them as bottom feeders to work for those at the top. Eventually, morality and political actions will restrict oppressive, greedy power. We must denounce gender, cultural, ethnic, and class walls. The reward is balance and equality for everyone.

Notes about Sparrow's Gift

A throwaway book *The Tongue-Cut Sparrow* from a library in my neighborhood was a surprise gift, a picture book about Shinto beliefs, which I used in storytelling tours the Japanese Gallery at the Asia Art Museum. The book was in the trash; I understood why, from the Japanese traditional male perspective. He was the ruler of the house and government and jobs. He finally did the Shinto Sparrow dance. Males married more than once; females were married off. The male point of view kept women enslaved through the centuries by loyalty.

* * *

I changed the narrative to two females to soften the harshness of the tale. I wanted the story to show the Shinto way of morality, the female's way. I told about the two grandmas while standing in front of a Shinto wood female statue from the eighth century that denoted feminine energies, the Komi force, the balance of nature, loyalty, and the gifts received.

The Tongue-cut Sparrow, which I renamed *Sparrow's Gifts,* informs about the Shinto beliefs, female energies, which were ancient and unwritten. The oldest records are from pieces of pottery showing birds that were the Tarii, spirits. The vital force is Komi, which is in all nature; everything is alive. To walk through the gate to Shinto, the medicine way, one must wash, then call the spirits, Tarii. The ancient believers called this the Honey Way.

11

Ursula, the Kitchen Princess embellished

Not too long ago, there lived Ursula, a young princess. As soon as Ursula walked, she went to the kitchen to help mix the porridges and stews, bake loaves of bread, and set the table for the servants and castle workers. She had a splendid time and loved Jenna, who was the head cook. When Ursula's mother died, Jenna became Ursula's replacement for her mother.

Ursula also loved the conversation in the kitchen at the serving table. She helped serve goblets of beer with meals—mostly stew or sausages. Satisfied and warmed, people talked about their position and what happened in their world.

The servant girls talked about the palace. Knights informed about news of other countries and the kingdom. The gardeners talked of their herbs and flowers and what took place in the garden, forests, and the animals they saw. The candle makers, the furniture makers, the ironsmiths, delivery boys…everyone ate in the kitchen and shared their news.

When the castle's tutor ate in the kitchen, Ursula asked him questions about the other kingdoms and foods. The knights and tutor discussed the salt wars. Ursula read books brought to her by the kitchen fire. She became wise and educated.

At dinner one night, her father, King Wilfred, announced to his three daughters, "My birthday is coming. A gift I want one from each of you fit for royalty. I will decide from these who will be the next queen."

Ursula was not exactly interested in being a queen because she loved cooking. A queen did not cook in the kitchen with servants. She would give her father a loaf of rye bread, sauerkraut, and sausages—his favorites. Ursula practiced and practiced. The carpenter helped her carve a wooden tray. She got exotic salt from the knights, who traveled to distant lands.

When her father's birthday came, she put the salt on the tray. The baked rye bread. Sausages and sauerkraut from the grill rested on a plate. The aromas were "perfect!"

From the dining room, rumbled, "Ursula. Ursula, get up here." *boom! boom!*

She carefully carried her tray, walking up the stairs from the kitchen. Father already wore the beautiful purple robe with gold and silver, which her oldest sister stitched. The jeweled wooden staff from her next sister, he pounded again. *Boom*!

"Where have you been?"

"Father, I'm sorry."

"Step closer! What do you have for me?"

She placed the tray on the table in front of him. He fingered the salt. He poked the sauerkraut, the sausages, and the small loaf of rye bread. "Is this... What is this? A wooden tray with salt spread around?"

"Dear Father, the tray is carved from wood, symbolizing the hearth, the fire in the kitchen where your meals are cooked."

"Why the salt?"

"Holy salt is a preserve, the Staff of Life, wars fought to own salt mines."

"What are you saying?"

"Our daily bread baked with salt, the cabbage fermented with salt, sausages flavored with salt. All for us to taste."

"Sausages, cabbage, bread! *SALT*?"

He pounded his staff. *Boom*! "This is what is important, a staff and a purple robe. These make..."

"No, Father, no! The robe only covers what you are. The staff makes noise. Salt is the Staff of Life! What people need…what brings us together. People must prepare and serve each other! To satisfy gives pleasure and brings prosperity, power."

Her father pushed the wooden tray away, glaring at Ursula.

"Your hair uncombed. Your dress covered with flour. Your hands and figure nails dirty. You're not royalty. Common, as common as the servants in our kitchen, go live with them."

Ursula ran to the kitchen into the arms of Jenna, "I can't stay here."

"My Father…"

"Yes, yes, I know."

"His rudeness! I must leave, live somewhere."

Jenna thought, "Well, I have my sister Greta who runs the Corner Road Inn."

"I can go there!"

"Greta serves food."

"That's perfect! Perfect! What I love!"

"Well…? I'm worried about your father."

"Father will be glad I'm gone. I can't go in this dress."

The servant girls knew the problems between Ursula and her father. One said, "I'll give you my dress." Another one offered, "You can have my hat." Another, "You can have my socks." Another, "I'll give you my shoes." Another, "You can have my coat."

Ursula blushed, "Thank you! Such caring friends." Then she cried. The kitchen staff hugged her.

Jenna said, "What you need right now is rest. In the morning, my husband Fritz travels you to Greta's."

Ursula went to her room, and she tried to rest.

Her sisters arrived and peeked at her.

"What you said was rude to father."

"We worked hard on those gifts."

"You did not! The servants did. You know that."

Upset, Ursula slammed the door. After many tears, she calmed herself, saying over and over, "I can leave. I can." Sleep did not come; Ursula was excited. She wrote a note to her father.

"Dear Royal King Wilfred, Father,
I'm going to live with ordinary people.
I'm going to cook what I want.
Ursula"

She folded the note and left her good-bye on the table.

Putting on the serving dress, hat, shoes, socks, and coat, Ursula ran downstairs, ready for the ride from her father's castle. In the kitchen were all the servants and workers who came to eat and talk, the friends she served. They hugged and thanked her, saying, "I will miss our Princess in the kitchen. You made us feel special."

She climbed into the wooden cart when Jenna ran from the kitchen. "Give this cabbage pie to Greta. The pie shows our love for each other."

Ursula carefully held the cabbage pie in her lap while the cart, pulled by a delivery horse with wooden wheels, bumped and shook. They traveled for hours until they came to a magnificent Corner Road Inn with horses tied and fancy carriages parked around the build.

Fritz pulled to the back. Ursula got out, stretching while Fritz pounded on the door. A beautiful woman opened the door. She had red hair, blue eyes, sparkling smile, and very robustly dressed with flour in her hair and on her hands.

Fritz said, "Jenna sent you a cabbage pie."

"My sister, oh, I've wondered about her and the princess."

"This is Ursula."

Greta observed Ursula, "Ursula! Umm! I've heard so much about you. The little Princess in the kitchen has grown."

Ursula blurted, "I've come to be your apprentice."

"My sister sent me an apprentice. Well, I have two gifts, the pie and the Princess."

When Ursula walked into the kitchen, she couldn't believe she was in a fantasy. Herbs hung here and there, as did sausages, jars of pickled vegetables, tubs full of spices and seeds on high shelves. Fish, poultry, and meats hung on hooks. Long tables supported workers who chopped, cut, and mixed.

Hanging in the large fireplace were pots with sauces, stews, vegetables, and pasta. Servers carrying trays of aromatic foods beautifully displayed left the kitchen. Then the servers arrived back with the empty dishes. At the same time, others washed pots, jars, bowls, silverware, plates, and goblets. Everyone moved in orderly chaos.

Greta observed Ursula. "Tomorrow, you start your education. Tonight go upstairs and rest. In the servants' quarters is a room for you. Take a bath; you had a long trip."

Early the next morning, Ursula ran to the kitchen, ready. Ursula learned as much as she could…"a little bit of this, a little bit of that, just right" and "so much oil, fry, turn over, be delicate."

Ursula asked the storytellers, troubadours, traders, and merchants eating with the kitchen staff questions about the countries they traveled. They told the news from east, north, west, and south, offering stories about the salt wars. They brought incredible foods: persimmons, nuts, oranges, and grains…turnips, cabbages, radishes, and exotic potatoes and tomatoes and corn from the new worlds. Ursula helped Greta create sumptuous dishes and offered them to her guests, who were delighted.

Ursula became an excellent cook, manager, and presenter. The merchants suggested to Ursula, "Why don't you offer services and cook outside the inn? We get requests from rich clients who have feasts and parties; they want special help."

Ursula blushed, "A marvelous suggestion adventures into the country."

Either traveling from the inn or staying in the owner's kitchens, Ursula organized fantastic festivals, feasts, weddings, and ceremonies. She became well known and sought, busily loving every minute, with not one regret.

Ursula's father heard about the catering service, and his letter arrived at the inn. Greta took the message to Ursula, saying, "Finally, a letter from your father."

Ursula studied the letter. "An apology from my father, no! He does not know where I am." She opened and read.

"Dear cooks of the Corner Road Inn:

We hear that you are traveling chefs, and we want to invite you to prepare our winter feast. I'm announcing one of my daughters as queen; the other daughter will be married to a king."

"We request that you stay; we have rooms. You may use our kitchen. Jenna is the head cook. Contact her.

With respect, King Wilfred"

Ursula, relieved, said, "Sounds like my father and an urge from Jenna. The invite is good, good…perfect. Greta, meet with my father and sign the contracts. Secretly, I'll go to the kitchen to prepare for the festival. I can see my kitchen friends who raised me, then father and my sisters." Greta agreed.

The catering staff packed wooden carts filled with beautiful dinnerware; exotic vegetables; various meats, poultry, and fruits; and unique ingredients: salt, spices, and herbs. The traveling went slowly and carefully.

When Ursula entered Jenna's kitchen, the kitchen staff, the knights, the pages, the servant girls, candle makers, bee handlers, gardeners, metalsmith, deliverymen, and merchants cheered their kitchen princess. They commented on her beauty and how glad they were to have the grown princess visit. Heartwarming and just, she felt loved.

The staff unpacked the linens' boxes, porcelain serving bowls, handblown glass goblets, silverware, bee-candle, linens, and unique spring garden greens.

Ursula went straight to work, unloading her supplies: pots, serving dishes, cutlery, platters, and serving ware. She immediately started arranging the kitchen and cooking with Jenna and the other cooks of the castle.

After two weeks of cooking, the setting up began. Beautiful, laced linens covered tables with white and blue porcelain plates and bowls, and hand-blown blue glass goblets, the house silver, and candles placed on top of the spring greens and the evergreens from the castle's garden with vases of spring flowers. Gorgeous were the tables!

On the day of the celebration, the guests arrived. King Wilfred entered, and behind him, the daughter to be queen and the daughter to be married. In a line, the royalty shook the hands of their guests. Ursula in the kitchen managing to ensure everything finished at the right time.

Guests and royalty sat around the tables, delighted with the spring flowers and greens displayed. First for the guests came wine, beers, meads with cheese and crackers, and cut vegetables. Then the champagne carefully poured.

King Wilfred stood wearing his purple robe and pounded his wooden staff…*boom, boom!* "Our festival is to celebrate my oldest daughter, who will become the next queen of our kingdom, and to my young daughter, who will become queen in the neighboring castle of King Albert in the West."

Everybody applauded and toasted "*Hurray!*" More champagne served all around the tables.

The first course came with baskets of varieties of loaves of bread, plates of cheese and butter, with jars of fruit jams. These cleared away, and the next course served was favorable soups, more loaves of bread, and pasta. Then roasted vegetables, roasted baby lambs, succulent pigs, spicy beef, grilled ducks, and quails with eggs. The savory dishes served in the blue and white porcelain bowls. More drinks merrily poured in the blue glass goblets.

To a server, the king demanded, "Do I get my royal dish that I requested?" The server bowed, saying, "Of course!"

Ursula, in the kitchen, knew precisely the royal dish. She retrieved the wooden tray she carved years ago from the hiding place, now cleaned and oiled. She spooned fresh, fine sea salt with tiny red specks on top of the tray, then smoothed carefully. On this she placed her perfect loaf of salted rye bread with a textured crust and perfect aroma. The sauerkraut was better than fantastic, having the right color and taste piled on a plate with tiny sausages spiced with sage and caraway seeds, both salted to perfection. Raising the wooden tray, her helpers in the kitchen applauded. "Please take the tray to King Wilfred." The kitchen assistant stood before King Wilfred and bowed. "This is from the chef."

The King recognized the tray, salt, sauerkraut, and sausages; he pounded his staff. *Boom! Boom! "The chef! Bring her right now."*

When Ursula heard his shouts, she slowly climbed the stairs confident and assured. Her father knew who she was. Ursula stepped before the king in her chef's clothing with flour on her hands and her hair and curtsied.

He stammered, "Ursula!"

He beat his staff, *boom, boom!* Standing, the king announced, "Friends, countrymen, family, I have a third announcement. Our excellent chef is

Ursula, my youngest daughter. Please, all stand and toast Ursula on her wonderful feast to honor her sisters. As she said, salt brings us together and now with her prosperity of fine cookery, gives us the gifts of life everyone deserves."

Cheers rang through the castle, as the court staff, kitchen staff, and the guests toasted Ursula. She blushed, recognized for her ambitions and efforts. Her father demanded, "Come, sit beside me, my daughter." Ursula knew her father's apology; he finally understood her love of serving. Long before this day, she forgave her father. Today, she won the prize—recognition.

He asked, "Please, stay here and be my chef, give us your finery."

"Thank you, father. I'm happy at the inn, and with my travels presenting feasts around the country. I will visit you and share the gossip and stories of my travels."

Life was fulfilled for Ursula, a kitchen princess, serving delicious meals to guests.

Today, we serve meals in our dining rooms to family or guests, and we share the saltshaker while conversing about our successes and travel.

Why demand recognition?

A girl princess stands up for what she wants. Ursula, our feminine damsel, loved to cook and spent all her time in the kitchen. Her father demanding and disagreeable with his youngest daughter, who preferred the kitchen and the servants, not an unkind king. Ursula will not concede and runs from the castle. At this time in Europe, the male and the social norms made "her" a victim to patriarch demands. Ursula does accomplish what she desires. A matron, an owner of an inn, helps her improve her skills in cooking and esteem. The damsel overcame her father's degrading language: "common as the servants."

When I was a youth, the role of servant demanded from women as daughters and wives. Luckily, I had a special dad who pushed me to take chances and adventures to save me from living the "damsel in distress." I saw my friends struggle and comply with the male codes and norms, which were strong in the city populated by the military, old farmers, or mine workers. I read traditional tales and recognized the servant standards. I could attend Colorado University. My education gave another view of male codes, how deeply rooted the traditional standards and norms ran in society.

12

Julnar of the Sea modified

Waiting to be found, I sat on an island in the sea. My brother was to marry me to a land king because of my anger. So he said—really, he wanted to save his kingdom.

With the first merchant that stopped, I bragged about my birthright and my wealth and education. He tried to rape me; I battled him off and swam into the sea.

After he sailed off, I crawled and waited. My uncle came in his boat. "I heard you ran away; I knew where to find you. Our Pomegranate Mermaid of the Sea."

I traveled for days with my uncle by camel to the Sultan Shahzeman, a monarch in Persia, in Ajam. The Sultan lived in the White City, his capital in Khorasan by the sea. He had one hundred concubines, yet none gave him an heir to inherit his fortunes.

I stood by my uncle, who said, "Sultan Shahzeman, my Sheikh, I am a merchant of the sea to sell this girl, who is more beautiful than any woman. Notice her marvelous figure, slender waist, voluptuous thighs, wrapped in silk veiled with gold to cover a face illuminated by beauty. Seven tresses of her black hair dangle in love locks, her deep black eyes, and heavy red lips. The sight causes longing for love."

In my dress of gold and silk, dangled with jewels, I held my body secretly and covered my face. I teased with my eyes. The Sheikh traced my beauty with his eyes.

The Sultan said, "How much for this maiden?"

"Two thousand ducats. We have traveled together across many seas and three thousand gold ducats pieces for my trouble. She is a virgin."

The Sultan tangled a bag of clinking golden coins in front of my uncle. "A gift to you merchant—here is a robe of honor and ten thousand ducats."

To his female servants, the Sultan said, "Bathe the maiden, adorn her, and furnish her in a bower where she will preside. Bring her everything she desires. Shut the door when you leave."

By a window looking at the sea, I planned to jump into the rocks to drown in the sea. I had no idea what to do. The Sultan came for his prize. I did not look or talk to him, not understanding his language. He stood entranced by my beauty. Slowly he sat beside me. He pressed me to his chest, "Your lips are sweet." I looked out the window at the sea, not speaking. I did not know his language.

He bowed and left me.

Again the next day and for weeks, he visited. "Has the maiden spoken?" He asked the servant girl. "*No!*"

The Sultan ordered lunch of foods I did not know. He ate and fed me. I did not resist.

"Silent maiden, your face is like the full moon or sun shining on a clear day. I thank Allah for bringing you."

He stood; always, he drew me near and kissed my lips. I remained silent, looking down with sadness. I used my silence to entice, and my youth and beauty profited me.

"Your lips are like honey."

For one full year, I did not speak. A silent, mysterious young concubine, dressed in silks and gold, played on Sultan's pride and his skills to seduce. I controlled the intimacy: his love grew. My silence enticed empowerment. I manipulated the control of my submission.

Again, the Sultan came, ordered lunch, we ate, and I said nothing. I remained quiet when he spoke. By now, I understood some of his words. He called slave girls to entertain us while he unrobed himself and then unrobed me. The silence of the captured maiden held respect, not lust.

I, Julnar, offered my best to gain wealth, respect, and honor with the birth of an heir for my family's esteem.

The Sultan said, "I am pleased to find you a virgin untouched by the hands of the merchant. I am devoted to your silence. I give up all my concubines; you are my favorite."

For days and weeks, he came, and I remained silent.

"I give my life to you, maiden. My entire world is yours. May almighty Allah favor me and soften your heart. My prayer is for you to grant me a son. For my great age, I require an heir for my kingdom."

I bowed my head for a long moment, looked into his eyes, and then smiled at the Sultan. I spoke, "Allah answered your prayers. I am with your child, and so I can speak to you."

Hearing my words, the Sultan danced and sang, ordering the servants to send 10,000 gold ducats to distribute to the poor in his kingdom.

"Why have you kept silent? What do you want?"

"I am broken heart. I am Julnar, Pomegranate of the Sea. My father descends from kings of the high seas. He died and left us his realm. While we grieved for him, other kings rose against us, our kingdom taken over. I quarreled with my brother, who wanted me to marry one of the kings. I raged, "I will never. My mother, Farashah; brother, Sahil; and sister, Dinarzada need your protection."

"Julnar, my kingdom, all I possess is yours. I love you. I'm to be your husband and you my queen."

I needed respect from my family. I had an heir, hopefully the sultan's son, which made my family part of his kingdom. A rejected sister to be a queen, I earned my acceptance. I owned my family's destiny; I had status!

"Dearest Sultan, I swam from the sea and sat on an island in the moonlight. A passerby found me and tried to rape me. I struck him on the head and hid in the sea. The merchant you paid for me was pious, virtuous, and loyal—my uncle."

"I want to climb to the rocks and slip into the sea. I'm ashamed; I am with your child. I will have no esteem, even if you were a Sultan. My family must witness your love and state of your kingdom."

"Oh, Julnar, the light of my life, if you leave, I will die."

"I need my family's respect for the birth of our child."

"How can your people arrive, if they're from the sea?"

"By the names engraved on the ring of Solomon, son of David, we walk and breathe as people on land. The animals, the moon, the sun, and the stars in the sky are the same as are the types of people. Mine are no different from the people here on this land."

"When I call my kin, you will tell them how you bought me with ten thousand gold ducats and treated me with kindness, honor, and the greatest respect."

I kindled a fire and threw aloe leaves on the flames. I held the ashes, whispering my language to summon my family.

"Worthy Shahzeman, you must hide. Look through the window. I want them to witness what you have given me, your wealth."

The smoke from the fire agitated the sea; the foam ignited and brought forth my brother, Sahil; my mother; my sister; and five daughters of the uncle, who was my merchant. They walked on water until they came to my door, where they entered.

My mother said, "For a year not eating, I longed for you."

My brother demanded, "You must come home with us; we need your marriage to a rivaling king."

I told them, "A sultan bought me for ten thousand gold ducats and gave up his concubines in devotion to me. Sultan Shahzeman has wealth and is a wise, good, generous man. He does not have an heir. I give him a son; I am treated with honor. If I leave him, he will perish, as he loves me. As you witness, I have the best of lives. The child I carry will inherit everything that belongs to Sultan Shahzeman."

My brother said, "Since you are happy, stay."

"I am happy, loved, and respected. I desired to stay with Shahzeman. He will raise our child; my love grows for the sultan each day."

I ordered a table set and supervised while the servant brought fruits and sweetmeats to my room. While eating, Sahil asked me, "We have not met your Sultan Shahzeman. We are in his palace and eat his food without permission from him. You praise him, yet he does not honor your family."

Sparks of fire entered the room from this assault against my Sultan Shahzeman.

Calmly, I opened the door to the closet. The Sultan Shahzeman came forth. "I heard everything and now I know how much Julnar loves me. Please, I welcome her family to my home."

Sultan Shahzeman ate with us. For thirty days, he entertained my family in his palace. Much later, after my family journey home, a son was born. Overjoyed, Sultan Shahzeman celebrated for seven days.

On the last day of the celebration, my brother Salih and my family traveled to name my son.

Salih held my child, penciled around and under his eyes, powdered his body, and anointed him with oils while reciting Solomon, son David, names.

He walked my baby into the sea. My Shahzeman wept. I assured him, "I love our son, who is safe. Salih will return."

Onshore, Salih handed Babra Basim, meaning "full moon," to his father Shahzeman. Then Sahil took a sealed box from his pocket, broke the seal, and displayed twelve jacinth emeralds, as large as eggs. "We are united with Julnar and you, Sultan Shahzeman; this is our gift."

"The twelve emeralds are worth more than my city."

"We are obliged to you. Sultan treated my sister, Julnar of the Sea, with kindness, honor, and respect."

After forty days, my family departed. Sultan Shahzeman loved me even more.

Babra Basim flourished in writing, reading, history, syntax, lexicography, spear throwing, archery, and horsemanship—education fit for a sultan. He was the charm of the kingdom. He rode around the city with this father and sat with Shahzeman in court.

My dear Sultan passed away. I received happiness and worth from my beloved Shahzeman, who respected my family. I have my son's good fortunes to attend. He is kind, ethical, and gracious as his father, and he needs a strong wife to help him.

◆◆◆◆◆

Why insist on respect?

Julnar sat on an island in the sea. She did not want to be given away to an avenging king; she desired respect, not married off for his family prominence. She was sensible, shrewd, unfaltering, and ceaseless, using silence and sex to make her unique, enticing a rich Sultan Shahzeman while insisting on respected love. Julnar controlled for love. Her manipulation of silence made her powerful and wealthy, gaining respect from her brother. Her family benefited as part of the sultan's kingdom; the shamed, rejected sister had status!

· ·◆·◆·◆·· ·

Blatant, shameless flirting, using beauty and body for sex—the apparent essential powers a woman possesses, used to gain her worth. I admire Julnar for using her feminine abilities to manipulate a man through seduction, although not what I would do, too dangerous, I would not move stuck as struggling mother. Julnar did the best for herself, gaining wealth, respect, honor, and an heir for her esteem and worth.

· ·◆·◆·◆·· ·

Women are captives in different situations and become accepting of their submission, making peace with their fate while longing for their distant dreams. Julnar worked her position for her good and maneuvered her desires to be real. As women, we need strong determination to manifest our dreams.

Notes about Julnar

This ancient tale involved a story within a story. The teller, Sacheherazade, had her motives for telling *Julnar of the Sea* from *1001 Arabian Nights*.

After finding out that his first wife, Sultana, deceived him, Sultan Shahrayar has her strangled. He swears to marry a different woman each night before killing her the following morning to prevent another betrayal. Sacheherazade, the Vizier's oldest daughter, concocts a plan to end his pattern of killings.

When King Shahrayar asked for the younger daughter, Dinarzada, her sister Sacheherazade, who was too old, too wise in philosophy, knowing medicines, fine arts, history, and a refined beauty, goes with her younger sister to spend the night. When King Shahrayar entered the chamber, Sacheherazade began a story. She stopped in the middle; King Shahrayar begged to hear the rest. Sacheherazade informs the sultan he must wait for the next night, thus saving both her sister and her. The next evening, Sacheherazade finished the story and began another, following the same pattern for 1,001 nights.

Sacheherazade, the brilliant storyteller, made her point to King Shahrayar in *Julnar of the Sea*. Julnar is similar to Sacheherazade, a woman who must save herself and still have respect. By the time Sacheherazade finishes telling all her stories during the 1,001 nights, she has three children by King Shahrayar and becomes the first queen.

"The oldest bit of Arabic text dates from the 800s; the first lengthy text was written in the 1400s. None of the early Arabic-language texts contains exactly the same stories. Scholars have identified Persian, Baghdadian, and Egyptian elements in the works, which seems to have developed over the years as an ever-changing collection of fairy tales, romances, fables, poems, legends about heroes, and humorous stories." www.encyclopedia.com

13

The Ruler of Birds intensified

Long ago, before us, when the animals could speak, all birds were crowded into the tree-of-life on a tiny island in the middle of the vast ocean. From sunrise to sundown, they squawked and squabbled…snatched food from each other…knocked down nests, and broke eggs.

Wise Mother Owl could not sleep. Her eyes were swollen, and she had a headache, "Who will stop this rumpus! I haven't slept since I hatched. Who will stop this arguing? *Who? Who?*"

Crow flew close to Mother Owl. "Birds can't."

"What, Crow?"

"We need a ruler!"

"No," said Mother Owl. "We need rules. Who will decide which bird is king without rules? Who will earn such an honor? Who will decide the rules?" insisted Mother Owl. "*Who? Who?*"

All the birds screeched at once why they could rule.

"Skylark has the sweetest voice."

"Nightingale sings the best song."

"Mockingbird has the most voices."

"Peacock grows the biggest plumes."

"Parrot wears the prettiest colors."

"Pheasant has the longest tail."

"Raven is the smartest."

"Vulture is the strongest."

"Robin listens the best."

"Hummingbird flies the fastest."

"*Squawk*!" Eagle swooped into the tree. "I have the sharpest talons. I demand respect. I will be Ruler of Birds."

Crow glared at Eagle, "Won't do! You need rules!"

Mother Owl said, "Eagle, what is important here is what makes us the same? Who knows?"

"We all sing," said Canary.

"We lay eggs," said Prairie Hen.

Little Wren flew next to Mother Owl. "Yes, Little Wren?"

"We have wings, and we fly."

All the birds squabbled and quarreled.

"I'm the fastest."

"I have the longest wings."

"I fly the farthest."

"I have the biggest wings."

"I can fly the highest."

"I'm best at soaring."

"I can stop in the air."

The big birds quarreled and squabbled and flew at each other, most rudely! The smaller birds tweeted, "We are not heard."

Crow insisted, "We need a contest."

The large birds cheered. The small birds protested that they were too small.

"Quiet! Order!" screeched Owl.

The chatter stopped.

Little Wren said, "Mother Owl, a flying contest. Whoever flies the highest and the longest will be ruler."

"Yes, Little Wren, a flying contest."

Crow directed, "Those wanting to be ruler, perch up along the lower branches."

Big and small birds crowded on the lower branches of the tree-of-life. To the ground, sank the limbs.

"QUIET!"

"NOW ready."

"Get set."

"FLY."

After the giant birds push off the branches, the smaller birds abruptly flung into the air…a mangle of wings pulling, which created a downward draft. Still, the birds flew up.

Mother Owl and Crow watched.

After an hour, the littlest birds tired.

After two hours, the middle-sized birds tired.

After three hours, the big birds strayed and rested in their roosts on the branches of the tree-of-life.

Soon most of the birds watched.

Only Hawk and Eagle matched flights. With a burst, Eagle soared high in the sky. Hawk fell below like a shadow. Then a speck jumped from Eagle, then both disappeared.

"A lost feather?" asked Crow.

"That is Wren, whose wings fly past the clouds," answered Owl.

After a long while, Eagle scooped into the tree.

"Not fair," screeched Eagle. "Wren cheats!"

All afternoon, the birds watched.

All night, the birds waited.

At daybreak, a speck appeared in the sky and floated gently to the highest branch of the tree-of-life.

"Little Wren wins," called Crow.

Eagle squalled, "I'm king! I flew the highest. Wren used my wings."

"What?" said Mother Owl, "Wren used brain power."

"Clever and quick! Little Wren is ruler!" shouted Crow.

"No! I flew the farthest. Eagle squawked. How far did Wren fly?"

"Look at my feathers," offered Little Wren.

Eagle squealed, "Dingy feathers are not royal dress."

"My jacket is scorched from brushing the sun. Our tree-of-life is on an island surrounded by water…a small dot. Our Earth is huge, decorated with wide oceans, long rivers, thick clouds, broad beaches, high cliffs, steep mountains, vast forests, and wide-open prairies. Trees, bushes, grasses, and flowers grow everywhere. Birds can nest in peace following these rules."

Eagle flew to the top of the tree-of-life to push Little Wren off. All the birds flocked around Eagle, screeching. Little Wren flew and perched between Crow and Owl.

"Order!" squawked Crow.

On their perches in the tree-of-life, the birds settled and quieted while they stared at Little Wren. Eagle stayed on his high perch.

Owl opened her eyes. "Who will honor Wren's rules?"

One by one, the small birds and the larger birds bowed to Little Wren. Even Hawk bowed. After some time with the others waiting, Eagle bowed his respect.

All the birds listened. "My rules are simple."

Ruler Wren considered each bird:

"Robins and Towhees live on the ground."

"Eagles and Hawks stay in the cliffs."

"Owls, Crows, and Peacocks nest in the trees."

"Quails, Doves, Jays, and Finches have the bushes."

"Ducks, Swans, Pelicans, Geese, and Coots live on the water."

"Seagulls and Sandpipers live on the beaches."

"While Turkeys, Meadowlarks, and Chickens live in the grasses."

"Sparrows, Swallows, Mockingbirds, Hummingbirds, and all small birds may nest anywhere among the trees and bushes."

The smaller birds nodded their heads with approval. Finally, all the birds cheered, "Long live Ruler Wren." Then each bird bowed good-bye to Mother Owl, Crow, and Ruler Wren and departed the tree-of-life to travel to their new homes.

Little Wren never wore a topknot for a crown or a robe of bright colors—only the singed, brown jacket—and nested near the ground in the bushes, never flying high again. To this day, Wren's tail points towards the sun to remind us who is the Ruler of Birds.

✦✦✦✦✦✦

Why seek equality?

My quest is for a qualified, creative, wise ruler, who understands and accepts that the feminists and damsels seek equality!

———————— ⁘✦✦⁘ ————————

A bird views Earth from above, offering a clearer understanding of what is on earth and to help everyone understand. In this ancient folktale, Little Wren gives rules to survive.

In the latest version of the tale, the winner is not the most robust, nor powerful; the winner is intelligent and wise. Wren's triumph is for all birds, who want space to fly and freedom to nest peacefully, as feminists quest for status.

———————— ⁘✦✦⁘ ————————

In Ireland and France, Little Wren is portrayed as a male king during the male-dominated social norms in literature from the sixth to eighteenth centuries. The appearance of wren does not indicate sex or gender. The female lays the eggs; both build and sit on the eggs, and both feed the chicks, much as humans who perform the same tasks of tending, feeding, and protecting the young. Birds and humans need to live without the harassment of domination. Acceptable social standards and rules need support to maintain who we are to stop the greedy bullies who want power and wealth. Further, we insist on equality and respect for males and females, regarding skin color, country born, jobs worked, health, and wealth.

Notes about Wren

*Bertha Rielly, a storyteller from Stagebridge.org in Oakland, California, is from Ireland and tells this story in her Irish accent. Since she knows the Irish background, she describes the use of a wren to ask for money from rich landlords by the poor peasants.

———————— ⁘✦✦⁘ ————————

Wren Day, "The origin may be the *Samhain* or *midwinter* sacrifice and/or celebration. The Celtic mythology considered the wren a symbol of the past year. The European wren is known for habits of singing even in mid-winter." wikipedia

"Wrann, Wrann, the Ruler of Birds" is a ballad:
"The wren, the wren, the King of all birds,
St. Stephen's Day was caught in the furze.
So up with the kettle and down with the pan,
and give us a penny to bury the wren."

◆◆◆◆◆◆

"Remember how in Ireland, a wren was considered the bringer of bad news, which is the role dedicated to crows and ravens in Slavic countries where a wren always brings good news? Did someone seriously misunderstand something here? I believe so. I believe that the old custom of killing crows and ravens on Winter Solstice…replaced with killing of wren."

December 27, 2016, *Old European Culture Blog*

◆◆◆◆◆◆

Fresno State, California: "The English legend that the wren is the king of birds has a parallel in German. A tale from the Brothers Grimm ("The Wren"/"Dier Zaunkonig," 1840, from Johann Jakob Nikolas Musaus) explains that, when the birds decided they needed a king, they decided to hold a contest. First, they said that the bird that could fly highest would be king. The eagle should have flown highest, but the wren rode on his back and so managed to climb higher. Then the birds decided to try a digging contest. The wren slipped down a convenient mouse hole, and won that round also. So the wren became the king."

"Vallancey claims that the wren was used in augury by the Druids, and so Christian missionaries hunted wren to prevent this use. (Hazlitt, p. 666) Flanders and Olney also date the story back to druidism."

◆◆◆◆◆◆

"Another story says that the tale will precede a future hero (e.g., King Arthur). Frazer compares the whole business to various coronation quests and hunts for sacred animals."

———— ✦✦✦✦✦ ————

"Greenway offers perhaps the greatest stretch of all, considering the wren to represent the "indomitable peasant." – RBW, Fresnostate Foklore

———— ✦✦✦✦✦ ————

Sir James George Frazier, *The Golden Bough: A Study in Magic and Religion,* 1922. The abridged 1978 MacMillan paperback edition explains the custom in Wales, the Isle of Man, and other parts of England; Simpson/Roud, p. 320. In a version in France boys beat the bushes for wrens: the first one to kill one is the king; the parading of the wren follows (Frazier, p. 623). Frazier compares the story to "the Gilyak procession with the bear, and the Indian one with the snake."

14

My original folktale, *Sylvia Saves the Day*

The sun, Myra, casts her fluorescent pastels of orange, pink, and gold rays over the hills into the morning. The colors span across the nightshades of browns, grays, and deep dark blues. The moon, Selena, along with her stars, nestles into the trees for rest.

Myra peeks into Sylvia's window.

The brightness wakes Sylvia, who walks to the porch. She wears the soft pastel colors of blue, green, purple, pink, and yellow of spring. Myra stretches to greet Sylvia, "Myra, my dearest friend, you bring the day."

Sylvia eats boiled oats and drinks elderberry juice on her porch while watching Myra climb higher into the sky over the garden.

Now and then, Sylvia watches Curran, the wind, ruffle and play in the clouds.

On this spring day, kittens play in the grass. Sylvia's dog with her puppies sleep on the porch, the birds build their nests in the trees, young squirrels play in the leaves, a cow feeds her calf, a ram plays with the lambs, the hens with their chicks scratch the ground while the rooster crows to the day, and a fox family spies from the woods.

As she collects her gardening tools, Sylvia watches Myra's warm light shine nourishment on the plants and trees for growth.

"Myra, your warmth moves the seedlings to stretch and face you. I till the soil of weeds, so the plants grow taller in your love."

Curran, the wind, dancing and laughing, blows the clouds into long strings of ripples.

"Myra, flowers open to you. I provide the energy of the spring water, so flowers stand strong in your radiance."

During the summer days, Myra enlivens the earth with bright cherry red, orange, yellow, green, purple, blue, and brown. Plants mature. Puppies, kittens, chicks, calves, goats, lambs, and birds with the animals from the woods become adults. They rest during the heat in the shade of the dappling trees of greens, yellows, and browns.

"Myra, you ripen the fruits and mature the vegetables for my table and the animals to eat."

In the distance, Sylvia studies Curran as he fluffs the clouds, ready to hide in the cool for a nap from the hot air.

During the autumn, Myra settles in the hills with shades of brown, dark orange, dark blue, purples, and dark greens spreading over the garden. Sylvia sits on her porch, petting her dog with her cat in her lap. The birds rest in the trees, and animals hunt in the woods or rest.

"Myra, as you rest behind the hills, I see Selena and her stars, our company during the warm fall evenings."

The leaves of the trees turn into the autumn colors of red, orange, and yellow. They fall and mingle with the browns of the earth. Gray molds creep and silence all growth in the garden. Cold struck!

Plants hide in the earth, birds take flight, and animals crawl into their winter homes. The cold traps Sylvia in her house; she preserves the garden's vegetables and dries herbs for the pending cold days. From her window, Sylvia searches the gray sky, "Myra, I miss you."

Curran blows his might against the hardening clouds to separate them.

Silver frost shines on the trees. Sylvia steps on her porch to observe the astounding beauty. Bites of bitter cold send Sylvia back inside her house for the heat of her fire. For days, Sylvia paints flowers, remembering the colors of warmth and the light Myra creates.

The gray fog blankets the valley and covers the garden and trees. Sylvia sees the damp curtain and shivers. "Myra, where are you?"

Curran begins his moan as he pushes the thick, sticking fog.

While Sylvia warms herself by the fire, the falling winter snow silences the warmth and colors from Myra. For one moment, Myra stretches through the thick fog towards Sylvia's window to peek inside. Myra loses her balance and falls into the woodpile. The cold freezes Myra. Sylvia looks from her window; she sees only the frozen earth.

For days, Curran's strains and wrestles the thick fog, which rushes back in thick whirling grays.

On these winter days, whites and grays and dark browns covered spring and summer. While Sylvia warmed herself by her fires, the rains cry from Myra. The tears freeze into snowflakes, which cover the ground, holding the world dormant.

Curran wails, searching for Myra; his tears drip and freeze into icicles. He roars and whips through the trees and valley; his anger bends the trees and rips the snow from their branches. Curran digs up brown-gray leaves, throws them into the clouds, and tosses them onto the frozen earth. In his rage, he blows Myra from the woodpile. Curran's anger binds him; he fails to see the faded disc. Myra sinks into his smothering battle.

Curran squalls against Sylvia's house. Her dog howls. Curran shrieks louder and louder. The trees moan under his grief. Cold gushes into Sylvia's home and moves her to build a hotter fire for the night.

When gathering firewood, Sylvia trips over a disc caught in the snow. Alarmed by the frozen face, Sylvia says, "Myra! My dear friend, without you, there will be no days. I will return you to the sky."

Curran storms at Sylvia. He blasts, "I do not trust you with Myra." Sylvia yells above the noise, "I found her. I will put her back into the sky." Curran roars, "I have the power and strength to blow Myra higher than your throw." Sylvia shouts back at Curran, "Yes, you are mighty…clear the clouds from the sky so Selena and her stars can light our way."

Sylvia cuddles her friend Myra as Curran blows the fog from the sky. The orange light of Selena and the star's bright blues streak across the long whites and grays. Animals appear from their hiding places, and birds watch from trees.

Then Curran rushes to Sylvia for Myra. Sylvia yells over his aggression, "Myra is also my friend. Take me to the meadow. I will throw our friend into the sky. You will blow her higher."

Curran roars around Sylvia as she stands in the mist in the meadow. He shouts, "Throw Myra up!"

"Be still!" shouts Sylvia. "There is not enough room; Myra is so frail she will shatter if she falls against the hardened earth." Curran pushes against Sylvia, "Throw Mira, now!"

Sylvia stands against his aggression, "Take me to the tallest tree."

Curran huffs around the tallest tree as Sylvia clings to a branch. She sees the whole valley as Selena, and all her stars light the sky. Curran howls, "The tree is the tallest. Throw Myra into the air! I'll push her up."

"Be still!" shouts Sylvia. "You shake the tree and make my throw impossible. My throw must be perfect. Take me to the widest lake."

Curran riles the water in the lake as he huffs, "Throw Myra high. I will catch her and blow her into the sky." Sylvia hesitates, "One mistake and Myra is trapped in the reflection of the lake. Curran, blow me to the highest mountain. Move fast; Myra is hot in my hands."

Curran blows around the tallest mountain in the valley. Sylvia balances on the top edge and braces her feet in the rocks, "Get ready, Curran, blow your strongest!" Sylvia casts her friend up. Curran catches Myra and lifts her beyond the night.

The sky floods with spring's pastels of pinks, blues, greens, and purples. "My dearest friend, Myra, again, you warm the day."

Curran carries Sylvia gently to her garden. He quietly floats into the remaining clouds in the sky. Sylvia walks to her front porch and rests in her favorite chair, marveling as the earth wakes to life.

+ + ♦ + + +

Why trust possibilities?

Curran is the male voice who pushes; he wants to save the damsel in distress. Sylvia needs the female sun for inspiration and growth; she protects the damsel in distress.

+ + ♦ + + +

I wrote this story in 1992 after my volunteer position as Regional Advisor for The Society of Children's Book Writers and Illustrators (SCBWI), from 1886 to1990.

I organized *Sylvia Saves the Day* as a picture book to have quilted squares for the twenty-seven scenes. The picture book never happened; I stopped illustrating and sending my stories to editors. The market dropped, and I waited in the vast valley.

After researching and publishing my father's family tree, which I call, *His, Her, and Ours,* in 1994, the family tree shook with the "struggling" norms.

Lying on my couch resting after rereading my written stories, a voice floated through my mind, "You write analogies. You need the sunshine in the sky. Go dig in the rich earth so that you can move on." Gardening healed my hurts over my story rejections.

The lake was the reflection of norms I needed to overcome, to break free from them.

Well, as all events develop…while gardening during the cold rains of 1999, I developed pneumonia and had to stop weeding.

Again lying on my couch, the voice floated through my mind, "Time for you to stand on stage and tell stories." All my life, I never read out loud. At that time as Regional Advisor of Northern California for SCBWI, someone else stood and emceed the meetings. As a woman, female, she, or her, I worked behind the scenes as the server. This negative opinion stuck in my childhood belief. I needed the highest mountain to throw my desire into the vast sky, overcoming my doubts.

My opportunity arrived: to take storytelling classes offered at the Dominican University in San Rafael in 2000, a boarder education with an extensive range of stories than I read in fifth, sixth grades and junior high. After that intensive study, I was invited to tell stories at the Asian Art Museum in 2002. I entered the temples of stories and realized traditional male norms dominated stories—most times, females had no name. Also, the male narrative about his powers in folktales promoted esteem for male governments and religions. Always the power of the damsel owned by the male: the king, emperor, sultan, landlord, monarch, czar, kaiser, or clan, etc.

⁕⁕⁕⁕⁕

If I wanted to adjust the male narrative in my head, I must devise my female narrative.

15

I Will Do This Myself exaggerated from The Little Red Hen

Once upon a time, not so long ago, Prairie Hen sat on her nest of eggs in an open flat prairie, where the grasses were yummy. She thought: I bustle from my nest when I am hungry. I watch for gliding hawk or sliding snake while scratching for juicy bugs. I look for the sneaky bobcat when drinking. I listen for prowling fox while pecking the scattered seeds. Then, I scurry back to my eggs to keep them warm.

"*Cluck!* I need a better way to eat!"

Prairie Hen watched her chicks scratch for bugs and seeds while hiding under the thistle bushes. She thought: we check the grasses and listen for sounds of approaching danger, always aware. "*Cluck!* We need a better way to find our seeds."

One day with her chicks while scratching for seeds among the tall grasses, Prairie Hen heard, "*Swish! Swish!*" She squatted and squawked, "*Run, Run! Gliding hawk!*"

Looking up, she noticed wheat berries swaying in the wind and pecked the stock of seeds, which fell to the ground. Then she tucked seeds under my wing.

"*Cluck! Cluck, cluck!*" Prairie Hen called her chicks.

On the way, she met Ground Hog with all his uncles, aunts, cousins, brothers, sisters, sons, daughters, and grandchildren in their village on the hill.

"Hello, Ground Hog, will you help me plant these seeds?"

"Not I!" barked Ground Hog, "I like my hill. My family digs and eats the roots of the grasses." He chewed on a root as if the best food in the prairie. Then, he went inside his hole.

"Cluck! I'll plant these myself."

On walked Prairie Hen with her chicks along the path.

"*Boo!*" Jack Rabbit jumped in front of them.

She squawked. "*Hide! Fast! Run, chicks!*"

"I scared you!" chucked Jack Rabbit.

Her chicks came from the high grasses.

"Yes, you did, Jack Rabbit. Will you help me plant these seeds?"

"Not I!" said Jack Rabbit, "I like the sweet flowers and grass in the open field, where I can see." Off over the grasses, he hopped.

"*Cluck*! I'll plant these myself."

Prairie Hen and her chicks crossed the creek and met Musk Rat searching in the water and pulling up watercress.

"Hello, Musk Rat, will you help me plant these seeds?"

"Not I!" garbled Musk Rat. "I love eating the lettuce and the moss in my creek." Into the creek, she dived.

"*Cluck*! I'll do it myself."

As they approached the blackberry grove, Prairie Hen met Mrs. Mousy and her children eating green oat berries. "I'll help," squeaked Mrs. Mousy. "I am weary of hiding from gliding hawk, listening for prowling fox and wolf, watching for sneaking bobcat, and sliding snake."

"*Cluck*! Come to my home in the blackberry bushes."

Prairie Hen scratched holes into the earth while Mrs. Mousy nibbled the seeds from the stock. The mouse children placed the wheat berries into the holes, and the chicks scratched dirt over the seeds.

On a spring morning, Prairie Hen saw the new green sprouts.

She squawked, "*Cluck! Cluck! Bok! Bok!*"

On hearing Prairie Hen, Ground Hog, Jack Rabbit, Musk Rat, Mrs. Mousy, and her neighbors came running.

"BOK! Look, sprouts!"

Relived, everyone admired the tiny seedlings.

"Now, who will help care for the seedlings?"

"Not I." Chorused Ground Hog, Jack Rabbit, and Musk Rat.

Her neighbors grumbled, "Will take too long."

"*Cluck*! I'll care for seedlings with Mrs. Mousy."

All summer, the wheat grasses grew tall, taller, and taller. Prairie Hen and Mrs. Mousy also planted daisies, hollyhocks, and sunflowers. The children played and laughed while they carried water from the creek. The weeds dug were delicious. The juicy insects were dessert. The plants flowered and sweet fragrance jiggled in the air.

Just before autumn, the wheat flowers turned into plump green berries. "*Cluck! Sweet! Cluck! Delicious!*" Mrs. Mousy, the children, and Prairie Hen ate berries every day until full. At the end of autumn, the wheat berries turned golden and played rhythms with the wind, which called time to harvest the berries.

"*Cluck!* What to do?" Prairie Hen pecked a large stock that held berries.

"*Boom, crush! Bang!*"

"*Cluck!*"

Ground Hog, Jack Rabbit, and Musk Rat heard the thumping and banging and ran to investigate.

"Will you help harvest this grain?"

"Not I." Chorused Ground Hog, Jack Rabbit, and Musk Rat.

Her neighbors left, grumbling, "too dangerous."

"I'll do the harvest with Mrs. Mousy."

Prairie Hen noticed each berry had a chaff—a shell.

"*Cluck?* What to do, Mrs. Mousy?"

"We must take off the chaff."

Prairie Hen clucked to her friends,

"Who will help thresh this grain?"

"Not I." Chorused Ground Hog, Jack Rabbit, and Musk Rat.

Her neighbors yelled back, "Too messy."

"I'll do the chaffing with Mrs. Mousy."

Mrs. Mousy, her child, the chicks, and Prairie Hen danced on the wheat. *"Cluck! Fun!"* The wind blew the chaffs away in a big cloud. By this time, the golden berries were too dry and hard to eat.

Ground Hog, Jack Rabbit, Musk Rat, and the neighbors touched the dried berries. *"Rocks!"*

"Cluck? What to do Mrs. Mousy""

"We must break and grind the berries. I will save a few to plant in the spring."

"Who will help grind these berries?"

"Not I." Chorused Ground Hog, Jack Rabbit, and Musk Rat. The neighbors grumbled. "Do not know how."

"Then, I'll do the grinding with Mrs. Mousy."

"Cluck? What to do?"

One of the young roosters found a large plat stone. The other chicks found smaller rocks. On the large stone, we put the dry berries. With the rocks, they banged, mashed, crushed, and ground the berries into little bits. Finally, a coarse powder lay on the stones. Prairie Hen scooped the powder into a bark basket.

Mrs. Mousy said, "We made flour."

Ground Hog, Jack Rabbit, Musk Rat, and her neighbors touched the flour. *"Dust!"*

"B O K? What to do now, Mrs. Mousy?"

That is when a chick carrying water tripped, and the water splashed into the basket. *"BOK! Cluck, cluck?"* Mrs. Mousy mixed the water into the flour, which made stiff, slimy paste. *"Cluck*! We make dough."

Ground Hog, Jack Rabbit, Musk Rat, and her neighbors touched the dough. *"Mud?"*

"Will you help bake this dough into bread?"

"Not I." Chorused Ground Hog, Jack Rabbit, and Musk Rat.

The neighbors grumbled, "Won't work. Nonsense!" They went back to their homes.

"*Cluck*! I'll bake the dough with Mrs. Mousy."

Mrs. Mousy said, "The sun dries mud; we can dry the dough."

Prairie Hen laid sticky clumps of dough on hot stones, which baked the dough hard enough to hold."

While the dough baked bread, the chicks gathered sweet blackberries, Mrs. Mousy's husband brought honey to smooth on top of the bread. The baking aroma called to Ground Hog, Jack Rabbit, Musk Rat, their families, and her neighbors.

"Who will help eat these lovely loaves of bread?"

"I will!" answered Ground Hog, Jack Rabbit, Musk Rat, and all her neighbors.

"*BOK*! No, you will not. I found the seeds. Mrs. Mousy and I planted them and tended them while they grew. We harvested the grain, threshed the berries, and ground them into flour. Then we baked the dough into these lovely loaves of bread. Mrs. Mousy, her family, and my chicks will eat the bread."

"*Cluck*! What a feast we had!"

Mrs. Mousy and Prairie Hen have enough grain and bread for the long, cold winter. The snow piled deeper; finding food was impossible. Prairie Hen gave Ground Hog, Jack Rabbit, and Musk Rat pieces of bread for their hungry families.

When Mrs. Mousy and Prairie Hen planted the wheat berries in spring, Ground Hog, Jack Rabbit, and Musk Rat brought their families, and her neighbors came and helped.

"*Cluck*! We all had a good year."

✦✦✦✦✦

Why accomplish?

The Prairie Hen I heard as a child. I loved the fact that a little hen made bread all by herself. My Grandma Bessie was my Little Prairie Hen, who baked bread.

We did have prairie birds on the Alpine Meadows of Colorado, especially at Hartsel Flats, which we drove through to *go a fishin*. When driving through the plains, I saw the prairie hens nesting by the deserted settlers' wooden, dirt huts with grass roofs. Grandma Bessie walked behind a covered wagon from Indiana to Limon, Colorado, through these prairies. Then she lived in Colorado Springs near our home.

When my brother and I walked from our house on 18th Street across a long field to 26th Street to visit Grandma Bessie, we ventured through the disabled train terminal. Trains once traveled up Ute Pass to Cripple Creek to pick up gold. Then down the mountain to the Golden Cycle Mill, now abandoned. Across Fountain Creek that flowed below the Golden Cycle Mill was our home…now Freeway 24. What fun we had exploring the creek, railroad, and old mill!

By the time we arrived at Grandma's house, she had freshly baked bread waited for us, and we had many stories to tell her. Mean, cranky step-grandpa sat in his rocking chair demanding, and Grandma served him. He saved her and her four children when her husband died; my mom was six. My Grandma had a garden, cherry and apple trees, a pond full of fish, chickens, a goat, lots of cats, and six children. She made her bread in a wooden stove and had a water pump in her kitchen and an outside toilet. She did all this herself.

When we have a cause we might think is too hard for us, some of us ask for help. For the little hen story, I added a helper. They are out there. The prairie hen did what she did to make life easier for her and her chicks. I figured since Grandma Bessie did this in her world with male limits, I, her granddaughter, could accomplish in my world beyond male-dominant limits in the arts and writing.

In eighth grade, Mrs. Caldwell encouraged all her English students to write stories. I became an author…my first story published in a Colorado Springs Gazette newspaper called *Dog Comes Home*. Even then, I did not name my female dog.

I LOVE MY GRANDMA BESSIE, THE HEN THAT DID.

16

Li Chi, the Worm Slayer adapted

Li Chi had no brother and was the sixth and youngest daughter of a rice farmer who lived on a small farm in a dynasty in China.

Weeding the rice field with four sisters, Li Chi stopped to watch her father, mother, and oldest sister waiting. The ancient, rounded, bent sorceress and the tall, thin magistrate walked up the road with an ox-led cart. They wore gowns of silk embroidery flowers of golden and bright-colored threads. This day was the tenth day of the eighth month when a young maiden of fourteen years old offered to the eighty-meter worm that lived on the mountain. Li Chi knew the pain and tears of her oldest sister. Her family worked exceptionally hard, and this year the Sky and Earth Dragons provided five extra bags of rice to pay the bribe to the sorceress and the magistrate, saving her oldest sister.

Li Chi yelled, "That worm will never eat me, never!"

Since a baby, Li Chi heard stories about the eighty-meter long, hundred toothed, wide-eyed, rice barrel thick worm that slid down the mountain to eat chickens, pigs, sheep, oxen, and goats, sometimes farmers, and several times a magistrate.

Some years ago, a sorceress traveled into town. She informed, "In a dream, the worm asked for a young maiden aged fourteen to eat. The farmers must pay rice to save their daughters. If not having bags of rice or coins, the farmer gave a daughter as the sacrifice." Such pain went through the village.

Li Chi saw her father load the rice in the wooden cart. As sorceress and magistrate walked down the long, dusty road, her father, mother, and oldest sister bowed.

The next morning, Li Chi, eight years old, bowed to her father, "May I join you in the Tai Chi Ch'uan field dance."

He looked at his youngest, "No, I am a guard for our village; the dance is for male defense."

"Husband!" Mother stood by Li Chi, "We have no son, and Li Chi will be company for you." He grunted then bowed. Early every morning, Li Chi danced with her father. Li Chi became agile and fast.

Although Li Chi's family prayed and gave honor to the dragons, the Sky and Earth Dragons did not provide enough rice for the second, third, and fourth sisters. The sun was hot, and the rice dried. The sisters traveled by foot over the mountains to live with different aunts.

The sisters came back to help in the fields. The Rain and Earth Dragons provided for the fifth sister; Li Chi's father gave the sorceress and magistrate nine full bags of rice. Li Chi hated the sorceress and prayed daily to the dragons for their help.

This year, the rice shed needed to be cleaned. Li Chi worked stacking and folding the bags. Underneath the oldest bags, Li Chi found her father's sword.

Up early every morning before anyone else, Li Chi practiced. Plunging! Stabling, "I will kill the worm." Lunging, "The worm dies!" The sharp sword sliced into the dry rice straw. Sometimes she struck a bag of rice.

Her mother laughed, "The rats are big this year."

Li Chi turned fourteen; though tiny, she was strong, powerful, agile, and fast. Ready to kill the worm.

At dinner a few nights before the tenth day of the eighth month, Li Chi stood and bowed, "Father, Mother, my sisters, I will face the worm."

"No, Li Chi, no daughter of mine gives herself to the worm. The Sky and Earth dragons were good to us. We have the ten bags of rice to pay the sorceress and the magistrate."

"Father, you have six daughters and no son. We have no dowries for our marriages, and no one to take care of us when you die. We need the reward."

"No, the daughter of mine gives herself to the worm for a reward. Tomorrow, I take you to your aunt."

Li Chi ran to her room. Her sisters followed; they knew her determination. They knew the pain. They watched full of sadness as Li Chi put on her oldest work clothes and rugged, dirty boots. She grabbed her bed cloth and wrapped around herself. "I'm going to kill the worm." Tell father and mother; I will be back." Hugging her sisters, Li Chi said, "Pray to the dragons, especially the Black Dragon."

Li Chi rushed into the rice shed, declaring "Time for Father's sword." As she wrapped the sword in her bed cloth, Li Chi saw a small bag. "Rice cakes; I'll need these. Thanks, mother."

Down the road, Li Chi prayed as she ran, "Sky Dragons and Heavenly Dragons, especially the Queen Mother of the West, who birthed the first dragon; P'ngau, who made the earth; and his brothers who pull the Sun God's Chariot across the sky to grow our rice, help me kill the worm."

She ran to the far side of the village to the sorceress' house. "*Bang! Bang!*"

"Who bangs on my door at this time of night, so late?"

"Li Chi. I come for the reward!"

The door opens, "What did you say?"

"I've come for the reward for my father and sisters. I have come to give myself to the worm."

"What?"

Li Chi continued, "I also want a snake-eating guard dog, a large pot, bowl of honey, bag of rice, a flintstone, a silk gown, and leather boots."

"Slow down! Come in here! Wait in this back room."

Li Chi saw the door shut and heard the click of the lock.

As Li Chi waited, she practiced her dance and sword motions. She ate the rice cakes and prayed to the Red Fire Dragon for power, to the Yellow Earth Dragon for strength, to the Green Wood Dragon for protection, to the White Mental Dragon for wisdom, and to the Black Dragon for speed.

The tenth day of the eighth month arrived. Li Chi heard a dog bark and the magistrate's voice. "Where is she?" The door was unlatched.

The dog strained on his rope and growled at the sorceress.

Li Chi petted and calmed the dog. "I know you, the field guard dog. Strong and alert! You chase the snakes."

The magistrate handed Li Chi a cracked, rusted pot, moldy rice, hardened honey, and a broken flintstone. "You get no gown or boots—just a waste you will die."

"Where is the reward for my father and sisters?"

"The reward will be given soon enough," he scoffed.

Li Chi respectfully bowed to the magistrate. She packed the pot, rice, honey, and stone with the sword in her bed cloth and swung everything to her back. She bowed to the sorceress, "Which way to the mountain?"

"I'll walk with you, making sure you get there," spitted the sorceress.

Li Chi walked as fast as she could.

The sorceress panted and lagged. "Oh, hurry ahead, you are too eager for your death."

Following a slimy trail, Li Chi and the guard dog hiked up the steep, rocky path. Li Chi picked up sticks, "I'll use these for the fire."

Horrid smells blew down the mountain as they climbed.

About the middle of the day, the guard dog and Li Chi reached the top of the mountain. Scattered everywhere were bones. Li Chi and the dog heard growling and smelled rotten meat and rancid fat. The growls thickened as they entered a small stone temple with four columns under a roof.

Inside the temple was the mouth of a cave where the horrid worm slept.

The guard dog crouched at the entrance.

Moving slowly and quietly, Li Chi placed the sticks in the fire pit. She put honey and rice in the pot, situated the pot on the sticks, and sparked flames with the flintstone. She held the sword and crouched behind the fire. She prayed to all the dragons, "Give me strength, wisdom, and power to fight this horrid worm."

The smell of the melting honey and boiling rice circled into the air and clustered around the hideous stench of the worm's breath.

Li Chi studied the evil creature, which had a dull white color, not eighty, perhaps twenty meters long…half as round as a rice barrow, not hundreds…with maybe twenty teeth, short legs, no horns, no large fish eyes. The snoring stopped, the worm sniffed the air, then lunged towards the pot. Twisting back and forth with the hot pot, the honey with rice poured out, burning the worm's mouth and head.

The guard dog grabbed the serpent's neck, biting and chewing.

Li Chi lifted her sword and plunged. "One for my first sister, one for my second, my third, fourth, and fifth." The worm jerked and spun around. "This is for me!" She sliced his head. Then Li Chi stabbed the demon repeatedly for each maiden from the village he ate. *Pluck!* The evil slim fell to the floor, quivered, then silence…no breathing…dead.

Growling, the guard dog jumped off the limp mess. Li Chi watched the fire become ashes; she bowed and thanked each dragon for their help.

Then she crawled into the wretched cave and collected all the bones of the maidens. "What a waste of lives; the maidens did not fight the slimy worm. Their parents will be glad to set their daughters freed." She wrapped the bones in her bed cloth.

Climbing down the cliffs, they passed the sorceress' house. "Gone, everything gone!"

Arriving at the farm late in the evening, Li Chi's mother and sisters cried and held her. Li Chi's father stood proud and pleased.

Li Chi walked to the village in silence with her father. She rang the village bell, "*Gong, Gong!*" alerting the farmers to come to the village. Li Chi unwrapped the bones of their daughters. "I gathered the bones from the cave of the worm; may you and your daughters find peace." The villagers and farmers bowed to Li Chi and her father.

When the emperor came, he vanquished the magistrate, gave dowries to Li Chi's five sisters, and a reward of jewels to her father. He asked Li Chi to become one of his queens. "No, honored emperor, I work on my father's farm." He gave Li Chi gold for her dowry. Some years later, Li Chi married a farmer in the next village.

Today, a ballad is sung about brave Li Chi and her deed to save many, many maidens. May we fight bold as Li Chi did centuries ago for justice.

♦♦♦♦♦

Why achieve?

When I found Li Chi in the Asian Art Museum in the Chinese Storyteller's manual, I was elated—dancing and shouting, "Finally, a real heroine!" The legend is from the early Chinese Chin Dynasty, 265-420 BC. After the Black Dragon of 2000, who died unexpectedly and put China in flux, neighboring countries and different dynasties wanted power and competed for control of China. Li Chi's heroism happened eighteen hundred years ago.

As a girl child, my mother, bless her, helped. She pushed her daughter to believe in herself. My mom was a warrior; she worked outside the home for money against the social norms. She forced me to think of myself as a girl who could almost do anything she wanted. Then, in the 1960s, money make available for females of poor economic background to go to college. I was a woman with a future as a teacher, yet no recognition to be an author, artist, lawyer, doctor, film producer, judge, president, and on and on. My life still confined by the male narratives in fairytales and folktales and laws. Women as servant dominate and restrict literature past, present, and in the future.

Interestingly, words denoting the feminine always have a male word hovering inside. Always check the pronouns used and the narrator's writing or speaking; these pronouns are suppressors in our language.

   --> fe<u>male</u> second to a male
   --> <u>lad</u>y second to a lad
   --> wo<u>man</u> second to the man
   --> s<u>he</u> or <u>he</u>r second to he
   --> <u>hero</u>ine second the hero
   --> t<u>he</u>y has he included
   --> t<u>he</u>ir has he included

--> t<u>his</u> has his included
--> t<u>he</u> has he and can sound like he
--> t<u>he</u>se has he included
--> <u>he</u>r has he included
--> t<u>he</u>re has he and her

At least in Latin, the letter "a" denotes the female—the anima. The letters "us" denotes the male—the animus. Yin and Yang symbols for the equality between Chinese men and women are not true in the physical, possible only in spirit.

17

Durga, Who Saved the Gods with modified adaptations

In a valley of the Himalayas, three hundred earthly gods, fueled by Indra, God of the Heavens, anger, chanted, danced, and drummed…their desire to rid the heavens, Earth, and underworld of the horrid buffalo demon, Mahisha. Vishnu, the Preserver, awoke from his dreaming; Shiva, the Destroyer, from his meditation on his mountain; and Brahma, the Creator, emerged from his retreat in his cave.

The Hindu gods were in trouble.

The valley in the Himalayas shook with fire.

Rocks fell.

Wind roared.

Steam swooped from the earth.

BBOOOOMMMMmmmmmmmmm!

I stood among the gods, Durga, a mere woman.

Their anger created me.

All the gods stared.

"I come, the one and only from space, time, and sound. I come from the Mother Earth forces, with the voice of Shakti and body of Devi. I stand before the gods, as Durga, mere woman."

The gods stepped back.

I petted my lion, my mount.

I saw their admiration for me and understood their dread.

"Have no fear of a mere woman; Durga comes as a foe to evil. My duty is to protect the pure, the innocent, laws, and scriptures. The buffalo demon torments men and gods. I come to rid the heaven and earth of Mahisha. He is to return the nethers below my feet."

A horrid, evil buffalo demon came from the nethers and took over the underworld and Earth. The gods of the Earth walked with the humans, waiting for the demon to tire of his earthly pleasures. Instead, Mahisha, the horrid buffalo demon, pushed Indra, the Thousand-Eyed God, from the heavens. The horrid demon stole the heavenly palace with the poets, musicians, dancers, and songs. Indra's rage awoke the gods. The moment came to act.

I saw Vishnu and Shiva's relief. I felt the insult of Indra, who lost his temple. I knew the shame of the fire god, Angi, who, after years of worship and praise from the father of the Buffalo Demon, granted the boon that the Buffalo Demon would conquer the three worlds: heaven, earth, and the underworld. I knew Brahma's pain. After the demon stood on one leg, praying, for a thousand years, Brahma granted the Buffalo Demon a boon. The demon would not have immortality; only a mere woman could kill the horrid evil.

I felt the anguish in all the gods chased from their earthy temples.

"Durga, mere woman, appears to do my duty. I come from all of you. As I say, my duty is to protect the pure, the innocent, laws, and scriptures. I am part of you."

"Shiva, thank you, for my face and third eye,

Vishnu, thank you for my eight arms,

Brahma, thank you for my feet,

Surya, Sun God, thank you for my yellow skin,

God of Fate, my brown hair is healthy and shines.
Ocean of Milk, my pearls and red silks flow free.
Queen Snake, the strands of beads tie my clothing together.
Himaya, God of Mountains, thank you for my jewels and lion."

The Gods acknowledged and moved closer to me.
"Thank you for my weapons, my attributes:
God Indra of the thousand eyes, for your lightning rod.
God Vishnu, for your disc.
God of wealth, Kubera, for your club and bottle of nectar, which I tied
to my string of jewels for later use.
Heavenly architect, thank you for this axe.
God of Fire, Angi, for your spear.
God Shiva, for your trident.
God of destiny, for your shield.
God of water, Varuna, for the noose and shell."

I saw among the gods, two of lesser lights. I boosted my weapons and called
out in a horse yell. "I come to rid the heavens and earth of the Buffalo
Demon." The gods clapped, and flowers fell from the heavens. The two
lesser lights disappeared.

One thousand demons on elephants, horses, camels, and donkeys
stood on the mountain ridges. Two generals approached. "We are to fetch,
Durga, mere woman, for Conqueror Mahisha."

I glared at the generals. "I have come to rid these worlds of the Buffalo
Demon. He goes back to the nethers beneath my feet or dies."

With my breath, I squashed this army, leaving only one demon to tell
Mahisha.

Through the conch shell, I blew out my victory.
The worlds shook!

One thousand demons on elephants, horses, camels, and donkeys stood on
the mountain ridges. Two generals approached. "We are to fetch, Durga,
mere woman, for the Buffalo's chief queen."

I responded, "I come to rid these worlds of the Buffalo Demon. He goes back to the neathers beneath my feet or dies."

With my bow and hundreds of arrows, I crushed this army, leaving only one demon to tell Mahisha.

Through the conch shell, I blew out my victory.

The worlds shook!

Mahisha, as a wealthy, mighty warrior dressed in golden silks and jewels, swaggered before us. He carried a shield, ax, and spear. "Durga, mere woman, you of soft skin, curved hips and red lips, brown eyes, and flowing hair, be my only queen. We will rule as equals."

"Demon, you have not heard what I say. Return to the nethers beneath my feet or die." I positioned Destiny's shield and threw Indra's lightning rod at Mahisha.

The horrid demon knew I was his doom.

Mahisha turned into a raging buffalo and charged me.

My lion met him, and the demon turned into a lion and attacked by clawing. I threw the noose around the demon neck; he charged as an elephant with my lion wrapped in his trunk. I sliced off the elephant's trunk with the ax. My lion leaped to the ground, waiting; the demon charged as a buffalo. I threw Vishnu's discus at him.

Snorting, the buffalo dug into the earth with his hoofs, his horns ripping open the valley. Calmly standing back, I drank life's nectar; primal urge surged into me. My energy shook heaven and rumbled through the earth. My vision cleared.

The buffalo lowered his head and slowly charged. I raised my club and slammed the buffalo. As the buffalo stumbled, I jumped on his back, using the spear stabbed and stabbed. With the sword, I sliced off the buffalo's head. The horrid demon squirmed out the neck; I speared Shiva's trident through his heart.

The Buffalo Deamon, Mahisha, fell.

All was silent.

Then flowers showered from the heavens. Shouts of joy and laughter rang everywhere. I bowed. "My boon to all! Whenever you need me, *pray, chant, and dance.* I will come to protect."

As the gods clapped and shouted praises to me, I handed back their attributes, as they needed them to protect the innocent, laws, and scriptures. Then I quietly disappeared into the pools of the earth, ready to help any god or human, *just ask me.*

⋅⋅◆◆◆⋅⋅

Why use powers?

A mere woman controls men (gods, kings, and demons) while the man thinks he owns, as proven by one powerful Goddess Durga when called by the male gods. Her duty is to drive a demon from India. She has all the characteristics of a warrior: fearless, disciplined, determined, and physical powers.

⋅⋅◆◆◆⋅⋅

I met Durga when I was a child running across a field playing "Ya, ya, ya, you can't get me," teasing a monster. I did not know.

Years later, in a creative writing class, I wrote a short story of my childhood, enticing the monster. *"Nia yeah, Nia yeah, you can't catch us."* I fell; I knew the beast would suffocate me. When I stopped yelling and screaming, I saw this wonderful magical woman—not my mom, not an angel, not a faery, and not a saint.

I needed to protect my best friend, Joanie, who was molested and violated by her uncle. I told my warrior mother, who told Joanie's mother, and the uncle moved away. I eventually forgot the episode, knowing I was safe.

⋅⋅◆◆◆⋅⋅

At the Asia Art Gallery, preparing my stories, I met Durga again; only the male demon's voice shadowed hers. Finally, Durga, herself, spoke to me. "I am the field goddess you met as a child. I am of the Shakti energies of the earth, the Devi, the goddess of protection created by all the gods. Durga comes as a mere woman to help the innocent. You were a mere child, who thought a monster lived in the field. I conquer demons, help overcome foes, offer courage to stand and fight the evil."

I had my warrior, and Durga's voice, a strong she, her.

Her weapons are attributes of power: lightning rod, disc, club, bottle of nectar, a string of jewels, ax, spear, trident, shield, and conch shell. Symbols of capability, potential, control, authority, mastery, strength, vigor, persuasiveness are the female force of a mere woman. My damsel had permission to be strong, capable, and effective with my might. I can be a writer, artist, and storyteller with my voice in my own genre with my femininity. Strong women achieve; Durga is ready.

Notes about Durga

A statue of Durga, a Hindu goddess, is in the South Asian Gallery of the Asian Art Museum in San Francisco, California. Durga, Mahishasuramadini of Indonesia, Java, eleventh and twelfth centuries. Her statue is the last figure witnessed going out of temples; she protects.

The point of view telling the myth is Durga's, a mere woman, rather than the demon's point of view found in the AAM South Asian, Storytelling Core's binder.

The major and the minor gods create a powerful woman to conquer a demon, who requested a boon from Brahma, "death only by mere woman." I think the Buffalo Demon came from the Mesopotamia trade cultures many, many centuries ago to conquer India. The demon is part of the fights between the Hindu gods versus invaders. Demon Mahisha underestimated the Hindi view of women.

The gifts the gods give to the Durga tell how much the gods battled with outsiders to create immortality and status in India. The three hundred-plus gods absorbed into huge verbal "soap-operas," finally written into myths. I thought Greek mythology caused confusing.

Goddess Durga was the patriot goddess when India fought against the British for India's freedoms in 1947. Before Independence, Durga Puja celebrations motivate people to participate in the freedom struggle.

———————— ·•◆•◆•◆·· ————————

Pushed by the female warrior, I told Durga's story in the South Eastern Gallery in the Asian Art Museum in San Francisco in the children's storytelling program from 2002 to 2014, in 2003 at Bay Area Storytelling Festival, and at swaps, the 2005 Pacific Twilight Tales. I presented workshops *Durga and the Female Voice* to Asian Art Museum Core of Storytellers, Feather River Camp, Toastmasters, and Tell and Tellers Toastmasters, at parties and, in 2010, to the Women's Fireside Writers retreat at Asilomar, California, and for SAC's the Genre Tales called Myths and Fables told *Durga, Who Saved the Gods* on May 16, 2021.

———————— ·•◆•◆•◆·· ————————

I told my story of how I met Durga in *"scaring up the mean thing"* for the *American Has Talent* in a primary audition in the 2010…

———————— ·•◆•◆•◆·· ————————

The day was getting dark the right time, my friends and I stood on the edge of an abandoned city lot up the alley from my home and next to the Collin Kid's home. Six of us were "scaring up the mean thing" which was captured in the tall grasses full of crumpled-up paper dand the empty bottles. The mean thing couldn't escape. We tease, *"Nia yeah, Nia yeah Nia; you can't catch us."* Being young we could run fast, off I went. I leading out in front and all of a sudden I tripped over my feet and fell in the dirt.

My friend screamed by me. Alone with the monster, who was ready to pounce, I screamed and shouted. I twisted. I kicked the monster. It would not eat me. After a while I got tired and stopped to discover only dust flew around me. I cough then became quiet. I heard the crickets singing, I smelled sweetest flowers, and the stars sparkled. I was dusty and my knees leaked. I brushed them off. When I looked up, in a beautiful golden light stood a gorgeous lady dressed in yellow; she smiled at me. She was not my mother, not an angel, not a fairy. I stood up, brushed myself off, and walked across to my friends…waiting. They saw my dusty tears on my face, the dust all over my clothes and my scratched knees. Angrily I glared. *"No monster! No, mean thing!"* I walked down the ally; my brother ran after me. "What did you see?" I did not tell him, he might tell everyone.

✦✦✦✦✦

I did not include Durga or the rape of my friend, Joanie too personal for me, so my story did not appeal to the judges of *American Has Talent…* wrong venue.

18

The Bridge exaggerated from *The Billy Goats Gruff*

The times were lean, and the grass thin and dry, the Gruff family hungry. Small Sister Nanny, middle Brother Billy, and big Sister Nanny lived on a steep mountain in Norway with their father, Ram Gruff, and their mother, Ewe Gruff.

Every afternoon, the three young Gruffs walked to the cliff that looked into the deep rushing river. They stood on rugged rocks and longed for the tall colorful flowers and rich, green grasses growing in the meadow on the other side.

The young goats hoped the river would dry up. Their parents said, "The river never dried in their lifetime."

Many times, the big Sister Nanny jumped off the cliff into the river to swim to the other side; every time, the rushing stream took her far down the valley. Walking home was long, hot. She passed high-parched cliffs with caves of trolls who demanded gifts. Big Sister Nanny arrived home exhausted and hungry.

Today, as all days, the Gruffs looked across the river. Small Nanny longed for "A taste of sweet flowers." Middle Brother Billy wished for "A taste of the herbs." Big Sister Nanny sighed, "For a sweet crunch of the oat, rye, barley, and wheat berries."

Under cliffs in a cave lived the troll family. Father troll, his wife, and fourteen children were hungry. Mother troll looked across the river and desired the flowers, herbs, and seeds from the grasses. Times were lean for the angler and woodcutter; he would have a goat for his wife's pot.

Many times, Father troll built rafts from fallen trees ties together with dried grass ropes in hopes of paddle across the river. Always he traveled far down the valley. He walked back climbing cliffs and found caves of trolls who demanded gifts. He worked for these trolls arriving home exhausted and angry.

He listened to all of the Gruff's longings. He once jumped into the river and floated downstream. On one of his long trips through the gorge, he saw a bridge. He walked across the bridge and climbed up the mountain into the meadow across from his cave. He planned to build a bridge and eat the goats that came across.

The Gruff family watched the trolls weave a long grass rope from the last of the dried grass between the rocks on the cliffs. Father troll waited on the opposite side of the river. Then two trolls swung the rope line to Father troll, who caught the rope and fasten to the top of a tree across the river. All the troll children pull the rope with tree across the river. Father troll cut the bottom of the tree. *Snap!* The tree fell across the gorge. Three trees dropped across the river then rolled together, the trolls cut the short branches off the trees and tied them horizontally on top of the large extending trees. Then thin long trees laid and tied vertically over to the short tree branches made a path on top to cross the raging river.

Mother troll observed her children and their father happily building a bridge; she was delighted and would have her herbs and seeds.

Ready, the bridge stretched from the cliffs to the lush, green grasses in the meadows. The devious troll waited under the bridge. Mother troll asked, "Why not cross the bridge to the other side?"

Troll answered, "Not safe or strong enough for us." He said no more and sat, waiting.

After days pushed by hunger although Father troll waited under the bridge, the Gruffs decided, "Small Nanny Gruff would walk across first."

Small Nanny Gruff cried, "I am afraid of the rushing water. The mean troll sits under the bridge."

Big Sister Gruff said, "If he comes for you, tell him that your brother comes across next and is big and tasty. I will protect you if troll grabs you."

Middle Brother Billy Gruff added, "If you fall into the river, I will jump in and rescue you."

Over the bridge, the smallest Gruff crossed, "*Trip, Trap, Trip, Trap.*"

"*Who Tramps Over My Bridge?*" roared devious troll.

"Small Sister Nanny Gruff. I go to the meadow to make myself fat."

"No, you're not. I am going to gobble you up."

"Please don't eat me. I'm too little. Wait until my Brother Billy comes. He is bigger."

"Then be off with you. "Troll thought: I will wait until this goat gets fatter.

Minutes later, Brother Billy crossed the bridge.

"*Trip, Trap! Trip, Trap, Trip, Trap!*"

"*Who Tramps Over My Bridge?*" roared devious troll.

"Only Brother Billy Gruff. I go to the meadow to make myself fat."

"No, you're not. I am going to gobble you up."

"Please don't eat me. I'm too thin. Wait until my Big Sister Nanny comes. She is large and fat."

"Then be off with you." Troll thought; I can wait until this goat gets fatter.

Minutes later, Big Sister Nanny crossed the bridge.

"*Trip, Trap! Trip, Trap, Trip, Trap!*"

The bridge creaked and groaned under the weight of Big Sister Nanny.

"*Who Tramps Over My Bridge?*" growled devious troll.

"*Big Sister Nanny Gruff.*" Her voice was as loud as the troll's growl.

"*I'm Gobbling You Up.*"

"*Well, Come Along! I Got Two Horns And Four Hard Hooves. See What You Can Do!*"

Up climbed the mean, devious troll. With her horns, Big Sister Nanny butted him, hard. The troll grabbed her horns and screamed. Big Sister Nanny dangled him from the bridge over the rushing river.

Not what the mean, devious troll planned.

His children and wife heard his screams and ran to the bridge. "Husband, what are you doing?"

Middle Brother Billy Gruff said, "Your husband said he was to eat my big Sister Nanny."

"Dear husband, boil a tough goat? I want the herbs and grains, berries from the meadow. I thought you built the bridge for us to cross."

"As I said, the bridge is not safe," moaned the troll.

"Well, make the bridge safe and let the goats pay for their crossings. They go home every night."

The Gruff parents, Ram and Ewe, liked wife troll's suggestions, especially their children arriving home at night.

Big Sister Nanny Gruff pulled the troll from the water and tossed him to the cliff.

Every night, the young Gruffs brought Mother troll herbs, flowers, seeds, grains, and berries. The trolls ate well. Mother troll planted seeds along the cliffs. Father troll tended the bridge, and his children invented a watering system for their mother's garden. The cliffs came to life with the herbs and flowers. Many families moved on the cliffs and daily traveled to the meadow over troll's toll bridge.

The Gruff family prospered from the sale of their dry pastures for housing, and the trolls became wealthy from the tolls collected.

⋯✦✦✦⋯

Why be fearless?

In Nordic folklore, the trolls are the Valkyries; females who demanded warriors pay offerings to pass over the bridge to heaven. Written with many themes to motivate against tyranny, the troll became a male. His symbolized oppression and ownership illustrated by his words, "Who tramps over my bridge." Today's "trolls" ignore whom they entangle in greed for power. Goats are survivors of harsh climates—sure-footed, balanced, and flexible, able to climb precarious cliffs. Their "horns of plenty" fight enemies. The extorted knows not whom he extorts.

In our society, the negative norms sit under the bridges of opportunity to block, threaten, and discourage anyone from crossing over to prosper. For centuries, male-dominated sociolinguistics guard laws and attitudes to prevent passage over bridges to fertile lands: places to live, proper food, productive jobs, and just education.

Our voices are horns blown against troll norms for more just equality laws without cruelty, injustice, hardship, suffering, or servitude. Our horns demand bridges to freedoms and opportunities.

⋅⋅◆⋅⋅

The biggest Gruff is re-imaged in a female voice; women were equal warriors in the Nordic ages. Then I added the troll's wife, who knew compromises and understood hardships and offered a win-win.

19

Thoas and the Dragon embellished

Thoas lived in the ancient days of Greece in a village near Arcadia on the dry, wild, and lonely slopes of the northern mountains. As a young shepherd, he cared for his flock of sheep and goats.

Daily, up the steep canyons and cliffs, Thoas climbed with his sheep and goats to graze on the grasses. In the spring, the grass was green and juicy; in summer, the grass was parched and chewy. His goats and sheep were happy.

While the sheep and goats graze, Thoas observed the birds, insects, and lizards crawling around on the warm grounds and resting on hot rocks. He loved to hike among the rock and caves or sit still for hours observing the bears and the cubs. He looked for dragons, hearing they migrated to his mountains. He thought he saw them fly, only so far away; they looked like eagles.

This day on a very steep ledge, Thoas saw a creature, alone, which looked much like a long fat snake about two feet long with six short legs. The baby called *"chirp, chirp,"* a real dragon. She fell from her mother's lair.

He had a steep climb up a straight stonewall to get to the dragon on a small ledge. Steadying himself with one hand, his other hand searched for places to put his fingers in the rock to pull up. Slowly placing each foot in the next cracks, he reached the dragon.

Chirps turn to cries of despair; the dragon weakened from lack of food and water nearly dead. Thoas gently talked to the dying baby. Then calmly, he gently patted the dragon. Carefully, he placed her on his shoulders and slowly crawled down the rock to the path.

The sheep and goats cautiously watched the motionless creature. Thoas said, "Follow me, just a baby dragon. I'll take her down the cliffs to the river for a drink. She will fly home."

The sheep and goats trailed behind Thoas and the dragon. The baby wrapped her tail and legs around Thoas and purred. As they hiked down the trail, Thoas handed the baby bitter crabapples, grapes, herbs, and sweet berries to eat. At the river, she crawled from Thoas and slowly drank. "Go home, dear dragon. *Fly*! You will be safe at home."

The small dragon wrapped her tail around Thoas' legs. Chipping again for comfort, she stared into Thoas' eyes. "Dear dragon, I will take care of you until the time you must leave."

He carried the small dragon to his village. The shepherds, seeing the dragon, shouted to Thoas.

"Take that beast from our village."

"She will eat us all."

"The sheep are not safe."

The loud shouts from the angry male voices scared the dragon, which held tighter to Thoas. He could barely move. The dragon's chips turned panicky.

His father came running. Thoas begged, "Father, just for a while, until she is better. I'll take her back to the mountain when she can fly."

During the following days, the small dragon grew, as all dragons do. At first, dragon and Thoas slept in his cave on his bed. Growing more, she slept on the floor. Finally, they moved outside.

Of course, her appetite needed feeding. While watching his flock, he checked for food she might like. Luckily, this dragon breathed no fire. She did not fly either. Although she hid in caves, Thoas had to hunt for her.

The dragon rested on the cliffs while the sheep and goats munched on the grasses. The dragon seemed to talk to him in his mind, because he always knew what she wanted.

One day, she told him what she could remember. "I was in a lair with my mother and two male siblings when men in glowing armor and shining sticks took after my mother. She threw me off a cliff and went back to the lair for my brother, who I heard squalling. The men came from the lair with green dragon blood all over them. My mother, though broken, smashed the men with her tail. I found my brothers and mother motionless, dead."

"I ran and fell down onto the cliff. I was there for days until you found me. Thoas, thank you for the food and water. I will never hurt you."

The dragon's size and earthy smell scared the wolves and lions away from the sheep and the goat. Thoas did not see a single one since finding her.

The bigger the dragon became, the more the shepherds shouted their worries:

"There will be trouble."

"Dragons are dangerous."

"She might eat our sheep."

"She is too large, she needs to go."

"She will fly off with Thoas."

Thoas repeated, "She eats fruits, grapes, herbs, and olives, not meats. We will sleep away from the village in a cave. I will follow her every movement."

One day, his dragon said. "Thoas let me tell you why men are afraid of us. I am one of the earth dragons who tend the precious jewels and gold and silver ores for the Heavenly Emperor, who lives in the Far East over all the mountains."

At one time, man and dragon trusted each other as friends. A dragon befriended a greedy man; he always touched the jewels and amazed by the shining gold and silver. Aware of his ravenous eyes and thirsty fingers when he felt the treasures, she decided to test this man's loyalty.

The dragon said, "I am called to the Heavenly Emperor's palace; will you guard these treasures? I have a quest to make."

The dragon showed the man a chest. When opened, an egg appeared. "My treasures compared to this egg are nothing, which holds my life. If the egg breaks, I will die. Guard this egg with your life. I trust you."

The greedy man said, "I will die before any harm comes to this egg."

The dragon closed the chest and put the egg with the other treasures. She flew away from her lair.

The man's temptation for the treasure grew. "Dragons know not the treasures they keep. They are misers. I can save the treasure properly."

He broke the egg with his knife.

Startled by hot breath, the greedy man saw the dragon watching him. The broken shell lay empty. The dragon said, "I see how trustworthy a man is." Before the man could run from her lair, the dragon's rage tore him to pieces.

Thoas patted his dragon's head, "I heard that tale. The wicked dragon ate the man and threw his bones into the valley."

The dragon stroked Thoas, "We all see and hear what we want."

While Thoas rested in the hills with his dragon, one angry shepherd approached Thoas' father. "We can take no more. Dragons come down the mountains and devour whole flocks of sheep and sometimes the shepherds."

His father hesitated, "My son will know when to take his dragon back to the mountains."

The shepherds decided they would dispose of the dragon; they could not kill her to carry her far away. They plotted a special party for the village. At the party, they prepared a spirited drink of herbs and wine for Thoas and the dragon. The drug caused a deep sleep for both.

While Thoas and the dragon slept, they wrapped the dragon with blankets and ropes and put her in the cart that carried their wools to market. For two days and three nights, they traveled the dragon up the steep mountain over the top.

Thoas awoke to find the cart, the shepherds, and his dragon missing.

He ran to the mountain ledge where he had found the dragon. He looked and looked in all the canyons on all the cliffs and inside caves. Thoas became the saddest shepherd in the valley, not talking, not eating, and not watching his flock...always searching. She had vanished.

Days later, the shepherds came back to the village with the cart. Thoas saw the blankets and ropes. He knew the men took his dragon. "You have killed her."

"We did not, we took her far over the mountains to the next mountains. Seeing other dragons in the sky, we hid and waited. Begging her not to eat us and pointing to the sky, we pushed her from the cart. The flying dragons fascinated her; we sneaked away."

"She will find her kind and possibly mate," comforted his father.

After a couple of months, Thoas tired of his hurting, anger, and longing for his dragon. "She is nowhere in the mountains. If she had to go, she knows where I am and will come anytime she wants." He watched his flock and made friends with other creatures in the canyons and cliffs, seemingly happier.

When Thoas calmed, his father asked, "Would you travel through the mountains with two older shepherds to sell our wools in a coastal city of Arcadia?" This offer perked up Thoas; he loved the market and watching everyone.

While in a tight valley of cliffs, six robbers approached and took the wools. Three robbers stayed to beat the shepherds. In horrible pain, Thoas screamed; his voice flew over the mountaintops.

From far away, his dragon heard his cries over the tips of the mountains into her lair. She flew out and over the mountains like raging steam. The terrified robbers run. She snatched each one, with mighty claws, smashed them into the rock walls.

Then she flew after the robbers with the cart of wools, snatched and clawed each to bits. She left the wool with the surviving shepherds. Thoas realized how terrifying she was.

The dragon lifted Thoas as gently as a newly born dragon and flew him to her lair. He observed three marvelous eggs in a nest; his dragon sat upon them. Her mate flew inside. He was as gentle as he was fearful.

"Thoas, I realized I could fly; I did not need wings, as the birds do. My power is in the notches on my nose. The other dragons taught me the skills."

"I am an Earth Dragon, now called Kua. As you see, my colors are brown and orange with bits of yellow. My job is to keep the Earth safe. My mate is a Sky Dragon, Yamen; he brings the rains. His colors, as you can see, are the blues and whites. We serve the Heavenly Dragons, which are golden and live in the Sky Palace. Water Dragons are green and dark blue and live in rivers, lakes, and seas to keep the waters safe. Fire Dragons are black and red and are the keepers of the treasures. We seldom see them."

"Where am I?" asked Thoas.

"You are far west of the sun and slight north of the moon, in a land where dragons dwell and live freely and with respect. Thoas, I mated with Yamen. You see; I have a clutch eggs."

She gently stroked Thoas. "I knew you loved me. I needed to live with my kind without fear."

Thoas stayed with his dragon. She offered fruits, herbs, and water until Thoas sturdy enough for his travel home. With care, Thoas saw when his dragon turned her eggs; she raised him with her claws. They flew to the place where the shepherds left her. "I have no grudge against the shepherds. I am happy."

Down the cliffs, Thoas climbed and followed the path to his village, greeted with cheers and hugs. He told the shepherds, "My dragon heard my screams and carried me somewhere to a faraway mountain to her lair. I saw her clutch of three eggs. She is happy."

Thoas never saw his dragon or her babies again. Every so often, he did see dragons flying above the mountains. Surely these were the children of his dragon that saved him.

Why utilize abilities?

My dream was to love a dragon, or save a dragon as in *Thoas and the Dragon*. Then I realized the dragon is myself, who I can love.

I changed the dragon to a "her" and added the eggs and lair. While nursed and loved in her lair, Thoas understood her rage while observing her loving care for her family. Finally, she could to share with Thoas, a man, her life as a dragon. She is a mythical creature, full of emotions, acceptance, skills, and acknowledgment. Both the dragon and the shepherd protected the other when becoming a victim.

Males used religious propaganda of hate and evil to suppress unfamiliar beliefs. In the twelfth to the twentieth centuries, male dominance "kept the faith" in literature, and in the sixteenth century burned women as witches to dismantle their healing arts.

After studying stories at the Asia Art Museum, I recognized the brutal killing by the Western cultures of the mythical East's beasts. Dragons slaughtered by Europeans because the Eastern culture sat on vast treasures protected by dynasties' dragons.

The story is an analogy for the treasures held: intelligence, feeling, compassion, reliability, and steadiness. Time to release the fanatical views of the traditional norms that women are hysterical, emotional wretches, helpless, or in rage. Women are strong, smart, warriors, business owners, inventors, and wealthy. Everyone can read, write, sign papers, vote, own land, teach, govern, serve, and advance thoughts and ideas. As males and females, as are peoples of color, we are the same, with similar ambitions mirrored by, through, and with each other, We are not dragons to be killed or captured for our treasurers.

Notes on Dragons

Dragons are ancient creatures. The first one born in China was Pa'gau, the creator of China and created the other dragons that float across the skies, swim through the water, and travel by land into our stories. Only the European Dragon had wings—most likely, the sails seen on traveling ships from China and possibly the Vikings' ships.

The dragon is in the Chinese Zodiac. And the first carving found on a rock from the eighth century BC. That is ancient. Supposedly, a tribe called themselves Dragons.

I have respect for the Chinese dragons, their history, and what they symbolize. I told *Dragons Shaped China* (to be a book) during my storytelling days at the Asian Art Museum in San Francisco. This book is a quick, brief history of dragons through eons and why each dragon was essential in creating China. Chinese dragons fly without wings.

20

The Farmer's Feast modified

Raven lived in the woods between the farmer's house and the deep forest. Raven helped herself to the farmer's food whenever she wanted. In her usual upright matter, Raven hopped in the creek, turning over stones looking for worms. Rooster crowed, "Come to Farmer Feast, all who are invited." Over and over, annoying Raven, she flew next to Rooster, who stood on the gatepost into the farm. "Rooster, why do you work for the farmer?"

"Well, I get food, safety, and prestige. You, Raven, are a thief. I saw you steal the farmer's corn. You are not invited. I gave a special invite to all the animals with the best offerings for the farm." With those words, Rooster crowed and flew into the trees on the farm.

Raven turned to the farm to fly inside, when she heard a great rustling and looked at the woods. Here came Bear running along the road. Raven waited for Bear on an old stump by the gate. Bear, while not the smartest, was a good friend. "Why are you here, Bear?"

"I am invited to come to a feast, special for me. I am pleased and honored. I awoke early this morning to comb my hair, which is always messy."

"Your hair is thick and the most beautiful in the woods; you are invited for your thick full hair and rough skin."

"Bear stopped and looked at Raven.

"Don't go," cried Raven. "You will never come out, you have the fur that every human wants on their floor. You will be kept in a cage, then killed and skinned for your fur. I know; I see what the farmer does."

"Raven, you were not invited."

"The fur is yours, not mine. I have these black feathers, not good to anyone." Raven flew into the air.

Bear thought, "Raven is right." He turned from the gate and walked on the road through the woods back to his cave.

Squirrel came from the trees and jumped on the gate. Raven landed beside her. "Going to farmer's feast?"

Squirrel twitched her tail, not looking at Raven. "You do have a nice tail. The farmer wants nice tails like yours to clean up the dust in his house after roasting you on the pit fire."

Squirrel went on and on in a constant chatter, jumped from the gate, ran along the creek into the bushes, twitching her tail.

Mrs. Sheep trotted down the road, fluffed and proud. Raven flew in front of her.

"Oh, Raven, the ideal! I'm going to the farmer's feast and can't be messed."

"Your wool is clean and fluffy. This is why the farmer wants you to come to the feast—for your wool!"

"I know, my wool needs to be cut, and I am promised grains to eat."

"Mrs. Sheep, you will be locked in a barn. I saw that huge hollow dark space with stalls and pits for water and troths for food slop."

"Raven, you are jealous. You have only those back, hard feathers. I will be the judge of my life."

Raven moved and left the road to Mrs. Sheep.

While eating the seeds from the farmer's oats, Raven saw Miss Wolf creep through the grasses. Raven flew next to Miss Wolf, who jumped. "Why, sneak through the grasses?"

"What do you want? Raven."

"You're not going to the farmer's feast, are you?"

"Yes, I was invited, and farmer said I am useful."

"Miss Wolf, you see the farmer's dogs—in chains, behind a fence, begging for their meals. You want a life like that? You are a wild, fearless hunter, not meant to live in a wooden house in your own droppings. Surely, the farmer plans to use your hide for his blanket in the cold winter."

Miss Wolf studied Raven, "Do you really think that would happen? You are jealous; you were not invited."

"The choice is yours, not mine." With those words, Raven jumped into the air and flew off toward the dogs.

Miss Wolf stood a few moments, heard the dogs angrily barking, shivered, and then crept through the oats to the safety of the woods.

Raven sat on the gate, ruffled her feathers, and preened herself. Mr. Fox's tail bobbed in the grasses. Raven flew over to Mr. Fox, who, startled, yelped.

"Mr. Fox, you are charming in your coat of red that shines in the sun… a fine warm fur coat for the winter."

"Raven, yes, my coat is fine and warm in the winter."

"I'm speaking of the farmer's wife…a fine coat for her or a muff around her neck."

Mr. Fox glared at Raven, snubbed his nose, and pranced from the field back into the woods.

Proud Raven crowed; she saved four of her friends from the farmer.

Just then came Junior Pig, trotting on the trail by the creek, headed for the farm gate. Raven flew at him.

"Not a funny joke, Raven. Are you going to the farmer's feast? I've been invited to eat from his garden."

"Junior Pig, I do that anyway; no need to go to farmer's feast."

"You were not invited! A little jealous, are you?"

Junior Pig trotted on his way to the feast.

Horse pranced along the road. Raven flew in front of Horse. "Why so fast, and you look great—your main, your tail, and your coat, clean and shining."

"Can't chat; I'm invited to the farmer's feast. I can have all the sweet grains I want in exchange for my strength. Could not resist that invite. Don't want to miss any sweet grains."

"Horse, once you enter the gate, you will never gallop in the fields and through the woods again. You are stronger than the farmer, so he needs you to do his work and you will serve him all day."

Horse laughed, "I am stronger than a man; he can't keep me." Horse lowered his ears and pushed past Raven, who flew to the top of the barn and watched a rope flung over Horse's head, and a bit put between his teeth. Then Horse led by the farmer to the stables, and the door latched.

Raven waited on the gatepost; no animal came. She screeched and squawked with anger. Sheep looked from the barn behind a fence, and Junior Pig never heard busy eating leftover garbage. Raven flew to the orchard, picked the sweet cherries from the tree, and tossed them to the ground. She tore apart the strawberry plants.

Raven stopped her rage when Lady Cow and Son Calf crossed through the cherry trees. Lady wore a floral hat and a wreath of leaves around her neck, as did Son Calf.

"Lady Cow, where are you going?"

"Raven, you know about the farmer's feast. Are you going?"

"That farmer's hunger is so ravenous, he would pluck my feathers and cook me on his spit and eat me. I'm not going. I feast on what I want."

Lady Cow answered, "Suit yourself, Raven."

"Wait, once farmer tastes your milk, you will never leave and locked in a barn."

"No one will keep me or my child." With a toss of her head, outraged by Raven's words, Lady Cow bumped Raven out of her way with her horns.

Raven shook the gravel from her feathers and followed Lady Cow into the farm. She flew to the top rafters of the barn. Horse standing captive in a stall, and Mrs. Sheep locked in pen, as Junior Pig. Lady Cow with a rope around her neck led into the barn and separated from her Son Calf. With a rope around his neck led to the field by farmer. Raven heard Mrs. Cow and Son Calf's complaints. No one came. Raven was not big, nor strong enough to help. She flew to the gate to warn other friends.

Deer jumped next to the gate, scaring Raven. "Why so fast, Deer?"

"I'm to see the farmer and have a bit to eat, sweet flowers of all sorts, especially for me."

"Did farmer tell you this?" "Yes, in Rooster's invite. I'm a special one."

"Are you dumb, Deer? Sure you are special…for farmer's dinner. He does hunt you; better to have you in a cage for dining when he wants."

Hearing Raven's words, Deer jumped off the road and back into the trees and disappeared into the forest.

Next, Raven warned Old Goat, who said, "I'm too strong and I have my horns to protect me. And, what good am I to farmer? I have no skills and too old, not good to eat." Raven later saw Old Goat with bells around his neck tied to a cart, pulling buckets of milk from Lady Cow.

Cat jumped on the fence beside Raven. She purred, looking at Raven, "I'm asked to watch the barn. I hear full of fat rats and fine tasting mice. I must go; I am late. I can stay anywhere I choose."

Raven waited by the gate to see if friends left the farm. Cat arrived and talked to Raven, "I am very pleased with myself. I scratched the farmer. His family leaves me alone."

Raven sat in a tree screeching and squawking, noisily complaining about the injustice to her friends. After many weeks, she flew into the barn to talk to her lost friends.

Horse said to Raven, "Yes, I have a rope around my neck and a bit in my mouth, only to show me what way to move. I do not speak human language. Yes, I work hard for the farmer, helping him in his field and giving rides to the children. I get all the oats, wheat, and rye grass I can eat. No wolves to worry about; the barn is warm and safe. And, I graze in the fields. I have a wonderful life."

Lady Cow said to Raven, "Sure, I give the farmer milk. Farmer's wife makes butter and cheese; I earn special grains. Son Calf is happy in the field; he was too big for me to feed. I'm very satisfied, safe, and fed. No worries about the cold or the wolves."

Junior Pig told Raven, "Raven, you steal from the farmer. He lets me eat from the garden vegetable; I can walk all over the farm. Farmer's wife brings me scraps from the house. I am well treated and liked, so much better than rooting in the woods all day afraid of wolves."

Mrs. Sheep said to Raven, "You make up so much. I give my wool to the farmer, and feel so much lighter, and then I am washed. For my service, I eat fresh grass in the field, I have safety in the barn, and can talk to all the other animals."

Goat informed Raven, "The cart is nothing. I am strong, and farmer appreciates my help. Oh, the bell! I take Mrs. Sheep and Lady Cow to the field and this bell rings so the farmer knows where we are. When I bray for help, farmer comes with his gun. No worry about the dogs. They are in cages; he lets them out to chase the wolves."

Son Calf was in the pasture and had grown into a bull. "Raven, you are full of mistrust. Farmer is nice to me and I will give him many calves and heifers. I'm pleased with my life and I can eat all day in the sun in summer and have a warm barn in winter."

Raven, gravely disappointed, figured the animals too proud to admit they made mistakes. They had lied about being safe, warm, well fed, and pleased to serve the farmer. Raven said to Bear, Wolf, Mr. Fox, Deer, and Squirrel: "The others are tied in the barn at night and work hard during the day and given small portions to eat."

Today, Raven continues to fly free, nest, and eat where she wants.

✦✦✦✦✦

Why guard freedoms?

In the Farmer's Feast, the gender of birds and animals hard to identity, usually, they need a pronoun. I took my liberty as a storyteller to change the voice from *he* to *she*. Raven is a female narrator with *she* or *her* pronouns. Beware of what we assumed and absorbed through any narrative and pronouns used. The little boy as a narrator was not fitting, nor was a miller, who grins grains. I figured miss translations from the German.

As said before, I read all the folktales I could when a child. I biked to the West Side Library in Colorado City with my best friend, Marilyn. My reading scores went from a non-reader to excellent while, and I learned European and Middle Eastern cultures. Only, as I have said, the norm planted that only males narrate or wrote stories.

Raven, the female narrator, demonstrates she has freedom and has liberty; she flies. She eats what she wants, not tattered or fenced by a male farmer. She has concerns about her friends; she warns them, and some listen. We all have choices to make and the reasons why we do.

✦✦✦✦✦

My lesson is to watch and listen for male pronouns which announce their social norms, to recognize who speaks, what words used, and why said. Thanks to narrators who resist the negative norms and persist on recognition, worth, and value for everyone. Authors must state over and over again that social norms include everyone: all cultures and genders…our rights.

21

Turtle and the Hare an Aesop's fable enhanced

Jack Rabbit one day ridiculed Turtle: "Hey shorty, with these short legs… Your slow pace with that house on your back…You are as slow as a snail."

Turtle laughed. "Jack Rabbit, though you are swift as the wind with your long back legs, I could beat you in a race." The Hare believed Turtle's assertion to be simply impossible. Jack Rabbit laughed, "I challenge you the slowest of slow to a race. Turtle agreed. "A race to the finish."

Fox, who watched, offered, "I shall choose the course and fix the goal so all is fair." Both agreed. Other animals had suggestions for Fox, and finally, the course finished, so each had a fair and equal chance.

On the day appointed, Jack Rabbit and Turtle began from the line at the same time. Turtle never for a moment stopped her slow, steady pace straight to the goal.

Jack Rabbit played in the creek with the fish, and jumped in the grasses with the butterflies. He checked on Turtle to see where she was, slow and slower making him sleepy. Jack Rabbit laid down by the course waiting for Turtle and fell asleep. Turtle passed him and shook her head, "He is one over-confident rabbit."

Turtle slowly walked across the goal with no Jack Rabbit around, nowhere. The animals cheered for her. Still, no Jack Rabbit hopped to the goal. Tired of waiting, the animals went on with their business. Fatigued, Turtle tucked her feet and head into her house to wait.

Jack Rabbit, at last, woke up and jumped as fast as he could. He saw Turtle by the goal dozing comfortably dozing. He pounded on her shell.

Slowly Turtle peeked her head out, "Oh, Jack Rabbit, you are much faster than I am. Now you know how I accomplished: slow and steady wins the race."

••◆◆◆••

Why qualified?

My favorite fables, because I think of myself as a turtle, slow and steady, and somehow, finally, understanding what I know is true.

••◆◆◆••

When I was a child in Colorado, turtles walked on the prairies, and sometimes we caught one. The turtles were old; we never knew if they were male or female. I hope the slow, careful reptiles still walk on those vast plains of the Midwest and race with the long-legged hare.

••◆◆◆••

I have discovered the basic plots of traditional stories speak to our genetic bodies and connect to us. Writers and storytellers link these impressions into our spirits, psychic, and physical bones. We must use the female voices from our grandmothers and our mothers that resonate equality in our bones. As females, we can reimage time, scenes, place, characters, and events to enhance, resonate, and vitalize stories in a female voice of what happened for her. Today is the time for female storytellers and writers to reappraise the stories told before the twentieth century and recorded by male scribes to suit their values. The female—gal, woman, lady, crone, feminist, and girls—can win. We are qualified. We are writers, authors, artists, and tellers of stories equal to the man.

22

Damsels Survive Using Their Skills

While gardening in 1998, I became ill. I had to change my expectations of myself. My best friend Janet and I collaborated in professional landscaping for eight years. I met Janet in the late 1970s at meetings for in-house childcare. I ran a preschool for two to five-year-olds, including my children; about thirty other children attended over five years. Janet ran an after-school daycare. She handed me a book titled *The Dark Side of the Light Chasers* by Debbie Ford, published in 1998.

As far as I understand from Debbie Ford, knowledge about who we are and who we become is not the same for each being. The experiences we have, the attitudes accepted, and beliefs trusted impair successes in our lives. The attitude enforced by parents, schools, marriages, religions, professions, through social norms, we believed to be real.

My impairment was "males got everything." This attitude not from my dad, as fair as he was to me—this attitude came through my mother. Her brothers went to high school, not her. Her stepfather sent by my mother went off to work at age fourteen; she received no chance while her brothers granted privileges. My mom's stepdad's attitude greatly impacted me. My grandmother waited on this grumpy, bossy, older man. He lost his engineering career; he ran over a woman while courting my grandmother. She served this negative man, which affected my roots, my standing as a girl. I loved my grandmother as an inspiration…that she served.

The damsels in folktales enlightened progress for survival by their coping skills. Knowing and understanding their attitudes are gifts. Damsels used skills to overcome hardships. Today, the damsels' of folklore strengthen my journey through the male narrations in society.

My crippling attitude, lack of self-confidence

The working class holds harmful norms; for example, "life is a struggle, with work and more work," which coincided with "don't trust others," and "the rich white males' control." A fallacy passed from generation to generation, from hopeful immigrants to hardworking farmers, into the poor working class. A delusion hammered deep in my roots by male narratives accepted in society.

Confidence was the worst of the negatives. As Debbie Ford suggested, I asked the negative to appear as a personification so I could face, observe, and question confidence. An ugly, bent, aged man appeared, who slobbered. He had dirty hair, clothing, and fingernails. He glared into my eyes and heart. This same dirty man sold vegetables at the cattle auction when I was five. He offered me candy, which I took. He grabbed my arm and put his hand under my dress. My mother saved me. I shuffled into the car while the dirty man laugh; he won. I was stunned, guilty, and vandalized. Not only did he violated my body, he muted my voice; I made a mistake which destroyed my self-confidence. A deprived male insults the girl, declaring he knew more than I did about myself.

Years later, the same hideous man walked down the sidewalk and sat at my table at an outside cafe. I stared at his dirt and asked the analogized fear, "What do you offer?" He glared. I asked, "What is your gift?" He spoke no words. Courage swelled in my mind. I glared at sick, dirty, old man until he got up and walked away.

Then I charted my conversations with other negatives, the predators who festered prejudices and fears and hindered my productive progress.

Find the attitude and change.

The negative ATTITUDE is

____

Describe as a CHARACTER.

POSE/STANCE

VOICE

MOTIVE

What is this negative?

____

ASK? What am I offered?

____

Disconnect!

===

Positive ATTITUDE:

____

————————> **BREAK THE SPELL**

+++

MY GIFT IS "I AM OKAY."

Attitudes grow in sets

First, to move from the negative, I had to admit the emotion and attitude exists and had a balanced positive emotion. Fear is courage, silence is bravery, frozen is movement.

+ +◆+◆+ +

Second, I notice, when charting emotions about ten groups together, that these formed around each other, resembling an onion…from the inside leaves pushed to the top. As I changed the negatives into positives, long green leaves sprouted from the onion.

+ +◆+◆+ +

Third, attitudes that I resolved balancing positives with negatives pushed new leaves from the center. Then flowers pushed up and bloomed. When seed appeared, I picked them to spread my new attitude. Finally released, I cleared attitudes about my victimizing opinions from my childhood and young adult.

Weeds grow in our gardens

My concern was that other weeds would suffocate my garden.

When Janet I did the gardening, one of our observations was each client grew weeds that prospered in their garden. Living next door to each other, each client had different weeds. For example: "the should do," the unwanted grass; "mother's fault," the sour grass; "neglect," the giant messy dandelions. The client tossed their weeds into their gardens among their flowers. The negative emotions became real in physical gardens. Janet and I pulled and pulled—two women, one black and one white, working side-by-side equal in the gardens. With help from the owners, the weeds disappeared.

So, I looked for a weed in my garden. Horrors, I discovered the unwanted stink onions. While their leaves omit an odor as foul as the bulbs, the flowers smelled sweet. The onions grew among the roses and along my path coming into my house. The stink onion spread by small bulbs under the ground and caused severe crowding of the other plants, which called me for attention.

The stink onion seeds resembled pearls. I learned the pearls were associated with tears, regrets by decisions made, my annoyance that needed clearing. I also spread the pearls in other gardens as seeds; the flowers smelled sweet. I was a tool of oppression casting my negatives!

I hated myself; I let this happen. These stinky, multiplying aggressors—my negative "males own everything"—corrupted my writing and art space. I had a friend, Jackie, and we assured each other this happened in the art world. We were the proof, women left out, planting the negative deeper.

Burdensome, stressful, and tedious to remove, the troublesome bulbs showed no remorse, no guilt, and required digging, again and again, year after year. The work and constant watching caused an enormous demand; I planted the onions over a long time, sweet flowers with stink roots.

With patience, care, and persistence, daily I dug up the roots. Actually, in the end, a group of young African American males helped. They wanted work. Oh, yes, I did have the stink onions. I gave a nickel for each bulb removed or pearl found. The young men were also at odds with mainstream white male norms, rules, and standards. Finally, today, African Americans and feminists rewrite our social norms.

Attitudes build a BOX!

First, recognize the emotion fills the room: fear, joy, revenge, hate, anger, love, greed, hatred, and the projection of attitudes of struggle, negativism, fearfulness, blindness, selfishness, etc. These float around and crowd each other, demanding recognition and notice as weeds.

Second, children learn attitudes. At an early age, a child has little to remember and lots to learn, especially beliefs, opinions, and norms. The dry sponge soaking in views and ideas is enormous. The soaked judgments are dominant. The person thinks the attitude is correct, accurate, and makes right, to the destruction of clear thinking. This thinking blocks any reality suitable for us. The grown person strives to prove what the child believed correct through all living experiences.

Third, after repeated experiences, a child magnifies the grip on the negative position and limits possibilities. Get out of the child's picture, recognize attitudes, opinions, prejudices, and emotions; decide what you want and is best for your older being, now! Hug that child and take her or his hand; observe what he or she thinks. Change a limited vision for better opportunities.

Manage negative; get into the positive. "HER IS EQUAL TO HIM; WE BOTH OWN." Positive emotions, positive feelings, positive attitudes, and positive beliefs free deeply rooted negative ideas. My mom was a warrior in her way. She worked outside the home in a factory while doing all cleaning, shopping, and meal-making tasks. My dad did the male part of working as a mechanic, keeping the yard, car, and house repaired. Neither had an education; both handed me weeds mingled with their flowers as with the schools I attended, the male narratives I read, and social norms in my environment. Thanks to the skills of the damsels I absorbed by reading traditional tales, I understood survival.

<hr>

Venture into reality:

see, smell, observe, taste, and touch…react to the positives:

I am me.
She is not he.
He is him, his.
We live in balance.

<hr>

To all he, she, his, her, this, these, theirs:

-- > Get out of the BOX: observe, wonder, and marvel at the balance we have between the feminine and masculine.
-- > Get out of the rotten attitudes, start cleaning and weeding, decide what you want that is best for your child, youth, and adult. Change the norms for everyone.
-- > Work every day to encourage girls, maidens, matrons, and the crones; we have, we own. The genders will change the language and dismiss dominating negative narratives. A balance of social norms, standards, and laws, provides worth equality for each other.
-- > We balance; each is a being.

TO AND FOR OTHERS

I show empathy:
  I show encouragement,
  I show comfort,
  I stay level and aware,
  I am sensitive,
I LISTEN.

My concerns are:
  feeling relaxed,
  feeling free,
  feeling aware,
  having the highest
ESTEEM for the other and myself.

My concern is:
  relating being to being,
  adult to adult.

I own my feelings.
I own my being
(parent, adult, youth, child) (anima and animus).

I believe:
  The other has enough wisdom and knowledge.
  I expect the other to own reactions.

I trust and LET GO.

Bibliography

A list of sources for the folktales and legends selected for this collection of stories, *Damsels Overcome,* part of a series called *TIMELESS TALES TOLD.*

Many of the sources are from websites, history books, anthologies of tales: 1001 Arabian Nights, Arthurian Legends, Welch Mabinogion, Aesop's Fables, as well information form Wikipedia and videos on YouTube.

Others from the vast sources of notebooks, courses, and lectures in the Asian Art Museum Core of Storytellers from 2002 to 2014, where I told stories in the education program for children and on Sundays for adults at the Asian Art Museum in the Indian, Korean, Chinese, South East Asian, and Japanese galleries.

And many stories from books compiled during the twelfth to nineteenth centuries by Andrew Lang, Grimm Brothers, Peter Christian Asbjorsen, Ludwig Beckstein, and Hans Christian Andersen, which I read as a child, teenager, and in my later years as a storyteller. Their collections widened my view of history with various versions of fairytales, folktales, and legends that crossed over many countries for centuries.

From these, finally, I understand why the wicked stepmothers and damsels desired more and their longings to be queens and princesses... women starved for recognition and worth.

Naga Princess

Storyteller Manual for Southeast Asian Folktales, Vietnam, Asian Art Museum of San Francisco, 2002, pp. 23 - 24

I told this folktale in the South East Asian Gallery, 2004 – 2012 in my frame Anger and Forgiveness. The *Naga Princess* is one of Buddha's teaching tales.

Folktales from Vietnam, Under the Starfruit Tree, Alice M. Terada, Honolulu, University of Hawaii Press, 1989

Rabbit in the Moon

Magic Animals of Japan, Rabbit in the Moon, Davis Pratt and Elsa Kula, Berkeley, CA, Parnassus Press, 1967

Moon Lore, by Timothy Harley, [1885], at sacred-texts.com

"The moon rabbit legend is popular and part of local folklore throughout Asia. It may be found in diverse cultures in China, Japan, India, Korea, Sri Lanka, Cambodia, Thailand, Vietnam, and Myanmar." *Wikipedia*, Moon Rabbit - excellent!

In ancient Anglo-Saxon mythology Ostara is the rising sun, depicted with a Hare's head or ears that are associated with the spring and fertility and resurrection.

Spider Weaver

Tell Me a Story, The Weaver of Clouds, a Japanese legend told by Amy Friedman and Meredith Johnson, UExpress, November 07, 2004

The Spider Weaver (old story), Sayaka Watanabe, June 8, 2012

A version of this story can be found in the Japanese anthology *Konjaku Monogatarishū,* where the rabbit's companions are a fox and a monkey in *Folk Tales From Around The World.*

The Weaver Of Clouds (a Japanese legend)

YouTube video, *The Spider Weaver,* TET narrated by Brady Ketelsen, 10/7/2010. An old Japanese folktale set to classical music.

Little One-Inch & Other Japanese Children's Favorite Stories, by Florence Sakade and Yoshisuke Kurosaki, illustrator Yoshisuke Kurosaki, publisher, Tuttle Publishing

Florence Sakadeandlt-Bandgt was an experienced editor and author/compiler of many popular books on Japan. Her distinguished career spanned five decades, and she continued working until her death in 1999 at the age of 82. Yoshisuke Kurosaki (1905-1984) studied at the Kawabata Painting school and illustrated children's books from around 1927 until his death. His work has helped define the style of Japanese children's book illustration in the twentieth century.

Rice Goddess

Knowledge E website, LSCAC Conference Proceedings, *Female Liberation in Javanese Legend, Jaka Tarub*, given by Inayatul Fariha Nabhan F. Choiron. The nymph stripped of her powers to serve a man, lecture: what the stealing of the clothing/wings means to the women of Java.

An oral story *The Rice Goddess* told by Helen Mary Stein. In 2004 she heard the story from a young Javanese man that lived in a village by the Buddhist monument of Borobudur in Java.

Elisa and the Eleven Swans

The Eleven Wild Swans was written by Hans Christian Andersen, (1805-1875), and was translated from the Danish by M. R. James (1862-1936) as part of his *Hans Andersen Forty-Two Stories* (1930).

The tale was first published on October 2, 1838 as the first installment in *Andersen's Fairy Tales Told for Children, De Vilde Svaner* by C. A. Reitzel in Copenhagen, Denmark

Hans Andersen's Fairytales, translator by L. W. Kingland, illustrated by Rachel Birktt, Oxford Press, UK, 1985

Based on Folktales from Hans's childhood, Hans Andersen's, *Fairytales of Hans Christian Andersen*, collected by Neil Philipp, illustrator Isabelle Brent, Viking, 1985, pp. 28 to 42

The Wild Swans, Wikipedia

SDC, HC Anderson Centrel, *The Wild Swans,* Albani Torv 6, 5000 Odense "Jean Hersholt (1886-1956) was a Danish actor who emigrated to the United States, making himself a career in Hollywood from 1913. Then he was an avid collector of Andersen editions. Among other things, he translated Hans Christian Andersen's fairy tales and stories in the excellent edition, *The Complete Andersen* (six volumes, New York, 1949) which you may read on the web site, HC Anderson Centrel."

Enid's Narrative

Webmesh Global Network, "With an interest in ancient history enjoying a resurgence, you may find our section on ancient Briton of interest, you can read many ancient documents, from the Anglo Saxon chronicles through to the Magna Carta, as well as the *Welsh Mabinogion, Geraint son of Erbin.*"

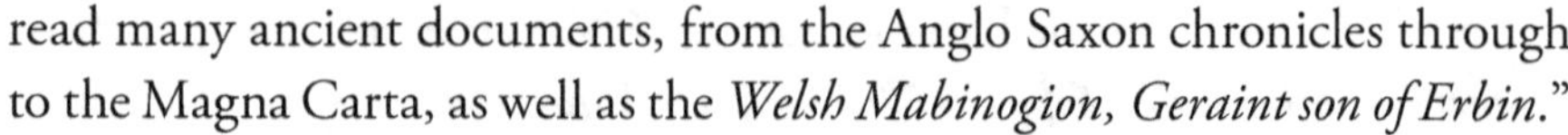

The Mabinogion "Geraint, Son of Erbin" from the *Welsh Mabinogion, the Primitive Celtic Arthurian Myths*, translated by Welch Lady Charlotte Guest into English in 1849. "The three-volume edition with English translation was printed by Llandovery in 1849, has been the English translation appearing in an edition of 1879. The Welsh text was printed in a diplomatic edition, *The Red Book of Hergest* by J. Rhys and J. Gwenogfryn Evans (Oxford, 1887). Lady Guest's translation has been re-edited with valuable notes by Alfred Nutt (London, 1902)."

Miss Gien, owner of the miaaglen.com says, "The stories are quite long. Therefore I have decided to cut them into readable pieces. *Geraint the son of Erbin* is in 24 readable parts." The legend is readable.

Geraint the Son of Erbin, website owner John Bruno Hare, March 4, 2004, pp. 141 to 184, *The Mabinogion,* translated by Lady Charlotte Guest, [1877] found at sacred-texts.com and *Notes to Geraint the Son of Erbin* and *Mabinogion History.*

Innocent Red

This story, *Little Red Riding Hood,* has many versions told as plots for novels and movies over many years. This story, told as a cautionary tale, existed before the Grimm Brothers, who wrote the story down in the eighteenth century. They mixed and matched story to suit their audiences.

The first known book with illustrations printed on carved wooden blocks. The *History of Little Red Riding Hood*, adorned with cuts, published by F. Houlston and Son, Wellington, Salop now known as Shropshire, 1810, for a penny. Collection of items about Little Red Riding Hood held by the British Library, #012806.de.29.(4.) #sthash.telQrN3w.dpuf.

Tatsuko, the Rainbow Dragon

Geisha, *Beyond the Painted Smile*, Asian Art Museum, Civic Center Plaza, San Francisco, CA, June 25 to September 25, 2014

The legend of Lake Tazawako - My friend Sarasa's mother lives by the lake and when I told her Tatsuko's story, she was overjoyed that anyone knew the Japanese story. She said that Tatsuko is still celebrated today.

Japanese Mythology, Juliet Piggott, Peter Bedrick Books, New York, 1982

Japanese Fairy Tales, Iwaya Sazanami, Hokuseido Press, 1938

Sparrow's Gift

Shitakiri Suzume, *The Tongue-cut Sparrow*, Mame-hon edition, text by Ippitsuan Kako, illustrated by Keisai Eisen, published by Yamamoto, 1844-47, 120×87mm, Collection of National Diet Library. The good man, his daughter, and the wicked, greedy female neighbor depict the Edo period in Japan, when men did the Sparrow Dance.

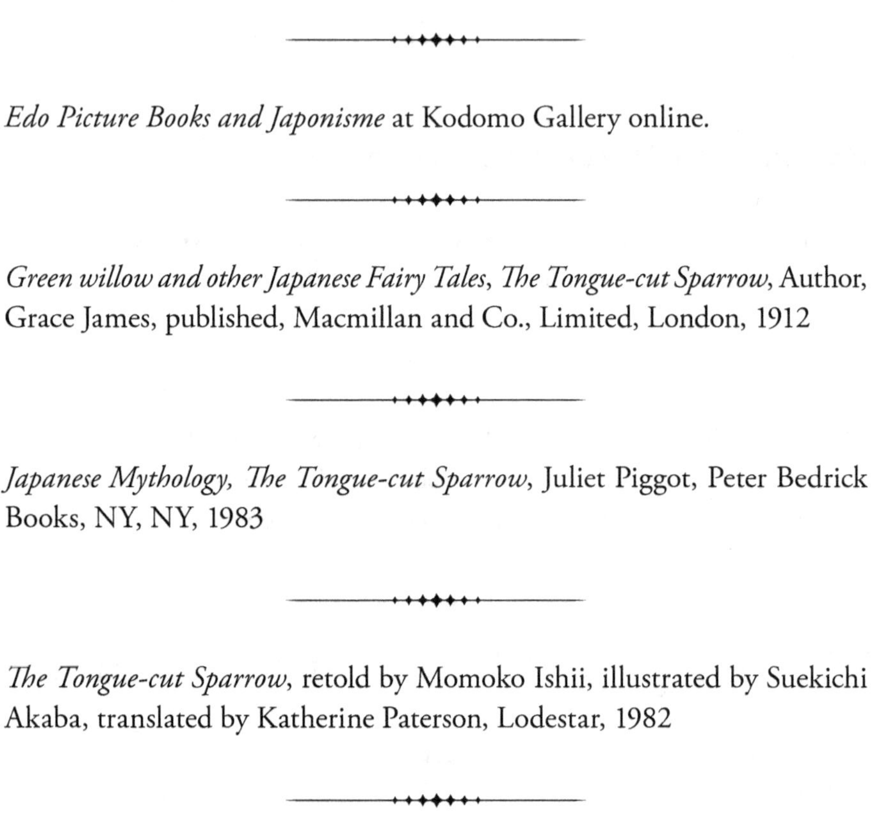

Edo Picture Books and Japonisme at Kodomo Gallery online.

Green willow and other Japanese Fairy Tales, The Tongue-cut Sparrow, Author, Grace James, published, Macmillan and Co., Limited, London, 1912

Japanese Mythology, The Tongue-cut Sparrow, Juliet Piggot, Peter Bedrick Books, NY, NY, 1983

The Tongue-cut Sparrow, retold by Momoko Ishii, illustrated by Suekichi Akaba, translated by Katherine Paterson, Lodestar, 1982

Ursula, the Kitchen Princess

The Most Indispensable Thing, Lugwig Beckstein, Samtliche Marchen, edited by Walter Scherf (Darmstadt: Wissenschaftliche Buchgesellschaft, Germany, 1983), pp. 593-596

© 1998 Ludwig Bechstein, *The Indispensable, New German Fairy Tale Book* (Leipzig: W. Einhorn's Verlag, 1856), Austria, Translated by D. L. Ashliman no. 24, pp. 171-75

© 1998 Bechstein's: *The Necessity of Salt* by Ignaz and Joseph Zingerle, 1852 Ignaz and Joseph Zingerle, *Necessity of Salt, Children's and Household Tales* (Innsbruck: Verlag der Wagner'schen Buchhandlung, 1852), Translated by D. L. Ashliman. No. 31, pp. 189-91

Ludwig Beckstein is the most popular editor and collector of fairy tales (1801-1860) and outsold Jacob and Wilhem Grimm.

The King and His Daughters, Charles Swynnerton, *Indian Nights' Entertainment*; or, Folk-Tales from the Upper Indus, Pakistan, (London: Elliot Stock, 1892), no. 27, pp. 78-79

Ursula and the Salt of Life – Bobbie Kinkead's telling on YouTube

Julnar or the Sea

The Arabian Nights edited by Katie Douglas Wiggin, and Nora Al Smith, 1856, 1876, illustration by Hayfield Parrish, who studied with Howard

Pyle, 1923, 1909, introduction by Mark Helprin, Harvard/Center of Middle Eastern Studies, 1947, *Gulnare of the Sea*, pp. 81 - 96

————————— ✦✦✦✦✦ —————————

Arabian Nights, The Thousand Nights and a Night, Classic Press, Incorporated, Santa Rosa, CA Andrew Lang, 1968

————————— ✦✦✦✦✦ —————————

Arab Folktales, translation by Inea Bushnaq, Pantheon Fairy Tales & Folklore Library, 1986

————————— ✦✦✦✦✦ —————————

The Arabian Nights - Chapter 23, *Julnar the Sea-Born and Her Son King Badr Basim of Persia,* author Sir Richard Francis Burton, 1885 from © 2005-2006 Thomson Gale, a part of the Thomson Corporation. All rights reserved.

————————— ✦✦✦✦✦ —————————

Halcyon Classic Series, 2010 Richard Burton (1821-1890) was the first European to reach many of the once-forbidden areas of the world, including many ancient Muslim cities. The British explorer, scholar, and adventurer had a gift for languages.

————————— ✦✦✦✦✦ —————————

Arabian Nights, Mimi TV Series, movie 2000, two hundred and fifty-five, "To cure a Prince's murderous madness, Scheherezade tells him a series of wonderous stories." IMOb TV

————————— ✦✦✦✦✦ —————————

Wren, the King of Birds

The Eagle and the Wren, Jane Goodall, illustrated by Alexander Reichstein, North-South Books, New York, NY, 2002

The King of Birds, Helen Ward, Millbrook Press, 1997

**The King of Birds*, Shirley Climo, illustrated by Ruth Heller, Thomas Y. Crowell, New York, NY, 1988. Both are friends of mine from The Society of Children's Book Writers and Illustrators (SCBWI).

Wikipedia - *Wren Days*

Robert B. Waltz and David G. Engle, California State University, hosts this site. *Folklore and Ballads* includes the ballad of *Wraan, Wraan, the King of Birds*.

Peter Fly and Fiona Somerset Fry, *A History of Ireland*, 1988 (1993 Barnes & Noble edition). "Starting in about 600 BC, Peter Somerset Fry and Fiona Somerset Fry present a concise and enjoyable history of Ireland taking the story up to the 1980s." A welcome introduction - Belfast Telegraph.

Sir James George Frazier, *The Golden Bough: A Study in Magic and Religion*, 1922, the abridged 1978 MacMillan paperback edition, Simpson/Roud, p. 320

Prairie Hen

Little Red Hen Makes Pizza, Philemon Sturges, ages four to eight, 2002. The little red hen shares her pizza with her friends. Philemon has reimagined and enhanced the ancient folktale.

La Gallinita Roja or The Little Red Hen by Lucinda McQueen, Paperback, 1995, also Easy-to-Read Folktales, ages four to eight, 1985, audio-cassettes available.

Little Red Hen, Byron Barton, 1993, an easy-read for young children and emergent readers.

The Little Red Hen, Paul Galdone, 1985, ages four to eight, available in video (eight minutes) by Weston Woods/Scholastic, Libraries

The Little Red Hen, Margot Zemack, Puffin Books, 1983

Li Chi, the Worm Slayer

The Serpent Slayer and Other Stories of Strong Women, retold by Katrin Tchona, illustrated by Trina Schart Hyman, Little, Brown & Company, 2000

———————— ✦✦✦ ————————

Li Chi Slay the Serpent, Chinese FairyTales & Folktales, translated and edited by Moss Rabitz from Kan Pao

———————— ✦✦✦ ————————

The Moon Maiden and Other Tales, retold by Hua Lony, a story from Chin Dynasty 265-420 BC

———————— ✦✦✦ ————————

The Serpent Slayer, Sweet and Sour, by Carol Kendall and Yao-Wen Li

———————— ✦✦✦ ————————

I told Li Chi's story in the Chinese Galleries of the Asia Art Museum to children's groups from 2002 to 2015. Her legend is included in my book, *Dragons Shaped China*. The boys enjoyed Li Chi's legend, as did the girls.

———————— ✦✦✦ ————————

Durga, Who Saved the Gods

Women in World History, Durga's Victory, Envisioning Power, 1996 to 2019

———————— ✦✦✦ ————————

Dolls of India/Durga – Goddess Durga: the Female Form as the Supreme Being

---

wikipedia - *Shankha/Durga*

Indian, Tibet and Himalayas, Southeast Asia Manual from the Core of Storytellers, Asian Art Museum in San Francisco, California, 2002

Workshops held at the 2010 Asian Art Museum, *Durga's Avatars, From Warrior Goddess to 20th Century Heroine*, Durga/Kali/Bharate Mata and Her Transformation, Mary-Ann Miller-Lutzer, September 3, 2010

---

wikipedia - Rebellion of 1857, Meerut: *The First War of Independence/The Great Indian Mutiny.*

August 14/15 1947, *Independence of India from Great Britain*

A statue of Durga, a Hindu Goddess, is in the South East Asian Gallery of the Asian Art Museum in San Francisco, California. Durga Mahishasuramadini, Indonesia, Java - eleventh and twelfth centuries.

The Bridge

The best website to research a story by Peter Christian Asbjorsen.

———————— ⊹⊹◆◆◆⊹⊹ ————————

Most storytelling of the Gruffs are in the form of picture books because the words have rhythm and action, as with cultural writings of the twelfth century, the old Nordic myths, all with male dominance and narratives.

———————— ⊹⊹◆◆◆⊹⊹ ————————

Anne Heiner, *SurLaLune Fairy Tales*, website, 2004, *The Three Billy Goats Gruff* was collected by Peter Christian Asbjorsen and Moe Jorgen.

———————— ⊹⊹◆◆◆⊹⊹ ————————

Popular Tales from the Norse, George Webbe Pasent, translator, Edinburgh: David Dougless, 1888

———————— ⊹⊹◆◆◆⊹⊹ ————————

The Three Billy Goats Gruff by Public Domain, Theo Kliros, illustrator, Harper Festival, 2003

———————— ⊹⊹◆◆◆⊹⊹ ————————

Mary Finch, *The Three Billy Goats Gruff*, Roberta Arenson, illustrator, Barefoot Books, 2001

———————— ⊹⊹◆◆◆⊹⊹ ————————

The Three Billy Goats Gruff, A Norwegian Folktale, SusaBlair, Pictures Ellen Appleby (Easy-to-Read) Scholastic, 1987

———————— ⊹⊹◆◆◆⊹⊹ ————————

The Three Billy Goats Gruff, Paul Galdone, Seabury Press, 1973

———————— ⊹⊹◆◆◆⊹⊹ ————————

Here is a gentle ending by Paul Galdone, 1973, having simple words and lovely illustrations:

> "So up climbed that mean, ugly Troll,
> and the big Billy Goat Gruff butted him with his horns,
> and he trampled him with his hard hooves,
> and he tossed him over the bridge into the rushing river."

Or, Paul Galdone in an earlier version taken from the 1880 Norwegian Folktale of Asbjorsen and Jorgen's telling:

> "Well, come along! I've got two spears, and I'll poke your
> eyeballs out at your ears. I've got besides two great,
> flat stones, and I'll crush you to bits, body, and bones."

Thoas and the Dragon

The Boy and the Dragon from *A Cavalcade of Dragons*, edited by Rodger Lancelyn Green, illustrated by Krystyna Turska, publisher Henry Z. Walck, Inc., New York, NY, 1970, pp. 11-15

Dragon stories are told and written by numerous people with various and different intrigues. I could not find Thoas anywhere, except in *A Cavalcade of Dragons.*

Farmer's Feast

1904, *The Brown Fairy Book*, '*How Some Wild Animals Become Tame Ones,*' collected and edited by Andrew Lang, published by eBooks@Adelaide, updated July 14, 2015, The University of Adelaide Library, South Australia 5005, pp. 156 to 159

Andrew Lang (March 31, 1844 - July 20, 1912) was a prolific Scott poet, novelist, and literary critic but is best known as a collector of folk and fairy tales. The Lang Fairy Books are a series of collections true and fictional stories he edited for children himself or his wife, Leonora Blanche Alleyne and other female translators published. Illustrations by Henry J. Ford, first published by Longmans, Green, and Co, 1889 and 1913. The books below found at Amazon.

THE FAIRY BOOKS:

> *The Blue Fairy Book* [1889]
> *The Red Fairy Book* [1890]
> *The Green Fairy Book* [1892]
> *The Yellow Fairy Book* [1894]
> *The Pink Fairy Book* [1897]
> *The Grey Fairy Book* [1900]
> *The Violet Fairy Book* [1901]
> *The Crimson Fairy Book* [1903]
> **The Brown Fairy Book* [1904]
> *The Orange Fairy Book* [1906]
> *The Olive Fairy Book* [1907]
> *The Lilac Fairy Book* [1910]

Hare and Turtle

1954, *Aesop's Fables*, *The Tortoise and the Hare*, translated by George Townsend, Baronet Books, p. 5, ebook from Gutenberg.org and #226 on the Perry Index.

————————— ✦✦✦✦✦ —————————

The coastal Indians of America have a story for the each thirteen sections on Turtle's back for the thirteen moons of the year. (Four stories on each side and five down the middle of the shell.) *Thirteen Moons on Turtle's Back*, Joseph Bruchac and Jonathan London, illustrated by Thomas Locker, The Putnam and Grosset Group, 1992.

————————— ✦✦✦✦✦ —————————

The turtle in Eastern mythology holds up the four directions of this earth. *P'ngau, the first dragon of China*, stood on Turtle's back and listened to all the stories Turtle told, who then gave them to the people.

————————— ✦✦✦✦✦ —————————

More Folktales, Legends, and Other Resources

The Oak and the Reeds, Aesop's Fable #70, compiled by Jerry Pinkey

————————— ✦✦✦✦✦ —————————

©1998, *The Dark Side of the Light Chasers, Reclaiming Your Power, Creativity, Brilliance, and Dreams*, Debbie Ford, Penguin Putman Inc., New York, pp. 185. Debbie Ford (October 1, 1955 – February 17, 2013) was an American self-help author, coach, lecturer and teacher.

————————— ✦✦✦✦✦ —————————

Sisters Choice, website, *'Active Heroines in Folktales'* Nancy Schimmel performed and taught storytelling in libraries, schools, and colleges throughout the United States since 1976.

+·+◆◆+·+

Fairytale/Folktale books, April 2020. Can only borrow Kindle, e-pubs, or PDF files from the University of Adelaide, the University of Adelaide Library, South Australia 5005. Last updated March 2016.

+·+◆◆+·+

© 1995, *Uppity Women of Ancient Times*, Vicki Leon and Ashala Lawler, Conari Press, Publishers Group West, Berkeley, CA, pp.161

+·+◆◆+·+

© Sept 5, 2020 *Dance of the Deities: Searching for Our Once and Future Egalitarian Society*, Patricia McBroom, Green Fire Press, PO Box 377, Housatonic, MD, 01236, pp. 164 "My memoir, *Dance of the Deities: Searching for Our Once and Future Egalitarian Society*, challenges male-biased academic narratives of human culture and evolution with evidence of female authority in ancient and modern egalitarian societies. Photos to illustrate the book can be found on my website:"

+·+◆◆+·+

©1993, The Woman's Encyclopedia of Myths and secrets, Barbara G. Walker, Harper & Row, Publishers, San Francisco, CA pp. 1124. "*The Woman's Encyclopedia of Myths and Secrets* has been criticized for being based on the idea of the "Great Mother" by male writers like Robert Graves and Erich Neumann, and for rewriting myths so they would support the theory of a "Great Goddess"."

+·+◆◆+·+

©1993, edited 2001 and 2004, Animal-Speak, The Spiritual & Magical Powers of Creatures Great & Small, Ted Andrews, Llewellyn Publication, St. Paul, Minnesota, pp. 383. "Teds Andrew, July 15, 1952 – October 24, 2009) was an American author and teacher of esoteric practices, and a clairvoyant."

Books Coming Soon
to Bookstores

Fire, the Hunger – The Humans do not listen when God Kaang warns about the dangers of FIRE, or Zeus' curse if they acquired FIRE. The humans destroy harmony that existed between the trees, animals, and men.

Sita's Narrative – Sita, the Goddess Lakshmi, the faithful wife of Rama told in the *Ramayana,* comes from the Hindu Heavens to save the world from Demon Ravana. Sita defeats this oppressor with her skills in her way.

The Taming of Tiger – Tiger, Guard of the West and King of the Beasts, when asked by Heavenly Prince to be the first man, leaves. After years of traveling, Tiger returns home to find Korea changed and Heavenly Prince gone.

How Dragons Shaped China – For eons, the dragons who lived in the sky, rivers, lakes, and in the mountains helped the farmer. Men then used the honor of the people for dragons to create great dynasties.

Pursued - Vasalisa, the Frog Princess – A dark, cold Fog crawled through the Elfin gardens searching and drowned the Elves' laughter. Seems Troll Caunte discovered his sister hid a Sherrie in her house. The Fog, ole Boneless, came for her.

Published:

RHYONNA'S FRIGHT

A Faery's Challenge to Save her Realm
© 2016 - Amazon and Smashwords

Grayed Creatures steal syrup from the BlackBerry Village leaving grayed fluff that eats everything sweet. Then Zzuf, a horrid parasite, captures Faery Rhyonna and spoils her wings. She must battle Zzuf to save her realm.

THANK YOU Story Coterie

My gratitude for your support, which enabled me to complete Damsels Overcome.

- To storytellers Bertha Reilly, Jean Ellisen, Penny Hiker, Emily Williams; Kelly Man, and swap leaders: Linda Walls for Mixed Bag, Marian Ferrante for Delta Weaves, Liz Nichols and Sally Holzman for TaleSpinners, and Ed Lewis and Sara Armstrong of SAC, Storytelling Association of California;
- To the board of CWC, California Writers Club for the mini book launch, June 19, and members: Francine Howard, Linda Brown, Lynn Fraley, Nancy Welch, Karma Bennett, Kristen Caven, and the writing and marketing groups;
- To the artists at Frank Bette Center for the Arts: Margaret Fago, Barbara DiSalvo, Pierrette Moore, and Rose Hoffman, and artists of AWA, Alameda Women Artist, Bonnie Boller and Joy Davis for a mini book lunch June 16;
- To Jocelyn Meggait proprietress of Free Up Oakland, art gallery, plants, and free items;
- To my family, friends, and neighbors: Sarah Knopp, Blake McNulty, Christa Buckingham, Joan Arnold, BJ Kinkead, Alex Norton, Carolina Juarez, Janet and Ronnie Murrel, Sharifah Sweet, Liz Rebensdorf, Eve Newell, my daughter, Brauley McNulty and grandsons Alessio and Costa, and my son Kirby and granddaughter Julia;
- To Judy Berne whose interview for Damsels appeared in the September 2021 community Rockridge News with over 5,000 readers.

CONNECTING . . .

I am pleased you read *Damsels Overcome*.

Send questions concerning the included folktales or legends to BobbieTales@gmail.com.

Go to my 'go-a-round' page BobbieTales.com, select the 'connecting. . .' button and leave a message or review.

For more stories, go to www.BobbieKinkead.com

Befriend me on my Facebook page BobbieTales - storytelling.

Follow me on Twitter@BobbieTales.

Read my blog: The STORY Realm.

AUTHOR

As a child, Bobbie Kinkead created stories: in the sand pile in her backyard, playing at the creek, hunting frogs, meeting the spirited folk; while catching grasshoppers as she walked to her grandmother's; and rocking in a swing on warm Colorado nights. As a teen, Bobbie rode her bike to the library to read every folk and fairy tale possible.

Graduating from Colorado University in Boulder, Bobbie taught first-grade in Anchorage, Alaska, then traveled to San Francisco to marry and taught art in the elementary schools. Moving to Oakland, she ran a home preschool where stories were important.

While her children attended school, Bobbie volunteered as Regional Adviser for the Society of Children's Book Writers and Illustrators (SCBWI) and editor of *galleys* for the Bay Area. As a professional gardener, Bobbie reconnected with the spirited folk and finished *Rhyonna's Fright*.

Attending Dominican University, Bobbie studied storytelling and asked to be a part of the Asian Art Museum (AAM) Core of Storytelling. Today she shares tales at swaps sponsored by the Storytelling Association of California (SAC).

As Bobbie explains, "...all important for writing a good story."

9 781942 070054